20 Underworld USA

# Underworld U.S.A.

Colin McArthur

The Viking Press
New York

The Cinema One series is published by
The Viking Press, Inc., in association with
the British Film Institute
Copyright © 1972 by Colin McArthur

Published in 1972 in a hardbound and paperbound
edition by
The Viking Press, Inc.
625 Madison Avenue, New York, N.Y. 10022

SBN 670–74064–0 (hardbound)
SBN 670–01953–4 (paperbound)

Library of Congress catalog card number: 72–75341

Printed and bound in Great Britain

# Contents

93902

# Introduction

The most interesting development in post-war film criticism has been the revaluation of the American cinema spearheaded by French critics, particularly those associated with *Cahiers du Cinéma*. The central critical purpose of the *Cahiers* group, and of their Anglo-American disciples such as *Movie* and Andrew Sarris, has been to demonstrate that *auteurs*, directors with consistent or developing views of the world expressed in discernibly personal styles, exist in the American cinema. Their critical method came to be referred to by the *Cahiers* group themselves as the *politique des auteurs*, usually translated as the '*auteur* theory'. Briefly, this started from the realisation that because the director in the American cinema was subject to a great deal more interference than his European counterpart – interference from stars, producers, writers, studio heads and so on – it was fruitless to attempt to discern the nature of the Hollywood director's art by considering his films as individual units. But by considering them together, the critic could sift the 'irrelevancies' brought to particular works by others and lay bare the core of recurrent thematic and stylistic motifs peculiar to the film-maker in question. This approach, doubtless implicit in the practice of critics in other countries, was – under *Cahiers'* polemical drive – enormously fruitful, deepening our responses to accepted artists like Alfred Hitchcock and Fritz Lang, and drawing our attention to the recurrent elements in

7

Hollywood looks at itself. Movie stars (Gene Kelly and Jean Hagen) at a film premiere in *Singin' in the Rain*

the work of younger directors like Nicholas Ray and Joseph Losey. Film culture in general owes a heavy debt of gratitude to the pioneers of this revaluation, and my own indebtedness is apparent in the chapters on individual directors in this book.

But the single-mindedness of the *auteur* critics, their exclusive preoccupation with personal authorship, caused them to neglect other elements in the Hollywood scene, most notably the force and function of the great genres, the Western, the gangster film/thriller, the musical, all of which throw up complex historical, economic, socio-cultural and aesthetic questions. This book is an attempt to describe the gangster film/thriller and the contribution of several directors to that form. My use of the term 'gangster film/thriller' calls for some explanation. Examples of both the gangster film and the thriller are readily identifiable: *The Public Enemy*, *Dillinger*, *The Big Heat*, *The St Valentine's Day Massacre* are gangster films; *The Maltese Falcon*, *Dead Reckoning*, *The Long Wait* and *A New Face in Hell* are thrillers. I argue that the two forms are very closely interrelated, particularly on the level of iconography, and that as both forms develop they often intertwine to produce films which structurally may be thrillers, but which carry much of the iconography and personnel of the gangster film (*Where the Sidewalk Ends*, *Out of the Past*, *Point Blank*). To complicate the picture, there are individual films, such as *Gilda*, *Double Indemnity*, *Lost Weekend* and *Sweet Smell of Success*, which are neither gangster films nor thrillers but which are variously related by mood, iconography or theme to both. Thus while it is possible to define individual gangster films and thrillers, the limits of each form are fluid; and the impression one has of the forty-year development of the gangster film/thriller is of a constantly growing amoeba assimilating the successive stages of its own development; or, to change the image, of a spectrum with the gangster film at one end, the thriller at the other, and an infinite number of gradations between them.

The structure of the book posed some problems. This is a

book about an aspect of the American cinema and not primarily about American social or cultural history. That is, I am interested principally in the themes and formal structures of the films themselves. To have written the book entirely around generic questions (e.g. one chapter on the several versions of the Al Capone story, another on the cycle of historical reconstructions of the late Fifties) would have taken me further into American social and cultural history than, in this book, I wanted to go. The present structure − four chapters about the genres, the remaining chapters about some directors who have worked within them − allowed me to sketch out my notion of the gangster film and the thriller and the relationship between them, and also to discuss in some detail a substantial number of films.

This book is in the nature of a holding operation. Despite the fact that Hollywood is now at the centre of informed critical debate in Britain, there is no serious, book-length account in English of any of the major genres. This book attempts to fill the gap as far as the gangster film and thriller is concerned. I have no doubt that as serious research in the field gets under way many of my conclusions and emphases, even on the historical level, will have to be revised. For example, we know very little about the several dozen gangster films (in addition to the handful I mention) made during the period 1930–32.

Questions remain. Whether, for instance, my perspective on genre, beginning the description from iconography, is the most useful one, or whether, as some critics have suggested, the background of reality should become the foreground and the cultural roots of genre be stressed rather than the formal properties.

Preparing this book has been an object lesson in the appalling neglect suffered by the American cinema from critics writing in English. Incredible as it may seem, there is no book-length study in English of the figures accorded individual chapters here (with the recent exceptions of Fritz Lang and Samuel Fuller). While there are excellent periodical and pamphlet studies of Don Siegel and Nicholas Ray, there is only the scantiest material on John Huston and Elia Kazan, a few random jottings on Jules Dassin, and no critical writing whatever (as far as I can trace) on Robert Siodmak. These facts reinforced my decision to structure the book as I have done.

If future critics can refine such perceptions as may be offered here, the book will have served its purpose.

# 1: Genre

In order to reach the reality of American cinema one must first confront the notion of Hollywood. If an audience, even (or perhaps especially) an educated and sophisticated one, were asked what Hollywood means to them, their replies would very likely include the words 'glossy', 'glamorous' and 'escapist'. They would probably offer the polarity of Hollywood movies equals 'entertainment', European movies equals 'art'; with the addition that discussion of Hollywood should be the province of the sociologist rather than the film critic. This view is held most widely in the United States itself. It is still difficult to find an educated American who takes Hollywood movies seriously. American undergraduates rush to see the latest Godard or Bergman, but if they go to see American movies at all it is usually in the spirit of viewing a lovable piece of *kitsch*, like the young Vassar girl in a recent novel who went to the Museum of Modern Art to take in a Bogart retrospective.

The reasons for this kind of educated response to Hollywood are not hard to trace. The most articulate writing about Hollywood, the fiction of Scott Fitzgerald, Nathanael West, Norman Mailer, Gavin Lambert and others, stresses the grotesque philistinism of the place, and there is a constant lament about how the art of the writer/intellectual is prostituted. Other cinema movements within America have reacted against what they believed to be the form or content of Hollywood movies:

thus the low-budget 'realism' movement of the mid-Fifties, based on New York television personnel, believed itself to be handling social issues in a more significant way than Hollywood, and the New York Underground Cinema has imagined that, by rejecting the technical excellence of Hollywood and confronting experience unmediated by narrative, it is producing more personal and vital cinema.

This rejection of Hollywood and its values, though understandable and even laudable, has led to a rejection of American movies which is neither. When one discusses literature or painting and, up to a point, drama, one can place the artist, his work and his audience in a very direct relationship. However, no such direct relationship with his work and his audience exists for the director working in Hollywood. There are at work several *modifiers of meaning*, factors which complicate these relationships. The most obvious are the star system and the subject of this book, genre – both, of course, partly explicable in terms of the overpoweringly commercial basis of Hollywood production. From the beginning, with very few exceptions, American movies have been controlled by businessmen. Lewis Jacobs, in his *The Rise of the American Film*, tells how movies were used by penny-arcade owners and vaudeville managers to turn a quick buck. When the growing film companies from 1910 onwards forsook the banks of the Hudson and moved to California, it was less in search of a particular quality of light than to escape the murderous patent wars back East; and the added incentive of California was less the quality of its landscapes than the proximity of the Mexican border over which bootleg cameras could be lugged. The subsequent development of Hollywood production may have changed in form, but not in its fundamental nature. If a company produces movies that no one goes to see it will go out of business; if a producer is consistently associated with films that do not show a profit, he will cease to produce; and if a director habitually turns out commercial flops he will cease to get assignments. The great mavericks of Hollywood, like Erich von Stroheim,

Genre as catalyst in the popular acceptance of *avant garde* impulses: surrealism in *Nightmare*

The influence of the gangster movie on 'high art'. James Cagney, Edward Woods and victim in *The Public Enemy*; and (opposite) Anthony Perkins and executioners in Welles's version of Kafka's *The Trial*

were men who could not work within their budgets and bring their movies in on time.

These are facts about Hollywood, but one should beware of making hasty deductions from them. Working from these facts, Anglo-American critics of the American cinema have traditionally evolved two critical syllogisms as follows:

(i) All commodities produced for a mass market are shoddy and inferior.

Hollywood movies are produced for a mass market.

Hollywood movies are shoddy and inferior.

This could be called the F. R. Leavis syllogism.

(ii) All great works of art are concerned with man in his social context.

Few Hollywood films are concerned with man in his social context.

Few Hollywood films are great works of art.

This could be called the Paul Rotha syllogism.

The first has led to neglect of and contempt for American movies among the notoriously over-literary Anglo-American intelligentsia; the second to such weird critical judgments as, for example, that the John Ford of *The Grapes of Wrath* is to be preferred to the John Ford of *My Darling Clementine* or, more generally, to the elevation of directors making overtly 'social' films at the expense of those working within more stylised genres.

Needless to say, the relationship between Hollywood's commercial structure and the meaning of Hollywood movies is more complex than either of these syllogisms suggests, and the influence of commerce has not been wholly or, arguably, even mainly for the worse. Simply as one example of the wealth of industry making possible the realisation of artistic vision, consider the area of technical development − deep focus photography, advances in sound recording, colour, wide-screen and so on. Also, while a reasonable critic must condemn the notorious Hollywood practice of producers interfering with directors' work, he must also accept the possibility that acts of interference may have benefited particular films. Nicholas Ray has described the front office interference with his plans for the making of *The James Brothers*:

My preliminary production scheme was to do the whole film on stage as a legend, with people coming in and out of areas of light, making it a period study of the behaviour of young people and the effects of war on the behaviour of young people, but doing it as if it were all a ballad. It meant never doing anything for realism, putting the realistic, but not the real, within a stylistic form to make a unified piece of work. This idea was accepted at one time during the preparation and again they got afraid of it and so the result was, I think, a very ordinary film.

If we look at the film as it now exists, particularly the magnificent Northfields raid sequence, we are compelled, in this instance, to thank God for the front office.

The emergence of genres in the American cinema belongs, up to a point, to the commercial nature of Hollywood production. There is a sense in which all Hollywood movies are genre pieces, there being in Hollywood a built-in impulse to reproduce a successful formula. Thus it is possible to classify Hollywood movies as sentimental comedies, social exposés, location thrillers and so on. But there are two genres which have been specially important in the development of Hollywood: the Western and the gangster film/thriller. Each genre has developed its own recurrent iconography and its own themes against which individual artists have counterpointed their personal vision, sometimes following closely the contours of the genres (as in the case of John Ford or Sam Peckinpah); sometimes finding in the non-naturalistic qualities of the genres a way of making their baroque sensibilities seem 'normal' or at least accessible to a wide audience (as in the case of Anthony Mann or Arthur Penn).*

---

* It is not only on the level of the individual director that genre acts as a catalyst between artist and audience, but also on the level of *avant-garde* ideas. For example, the American cinema has absorbed both Expressionism and Surrealism, habitually embedding both in genre movies. It is interesting to compare Luis Buñuel's *Un Chien Andalou* (1928) and Maxwell Shane's *Fear in the Night* (1947). The first would, very likely, be unwatchable by, and largely incomprehensible to, a popular audience; the second was made in Hollywood and played with moderate success in commercial cinemas in the United States and Britain. Yet, to a very great extent they carry precisely similar imagery (razors, sharp-pointed objects) and are about the same things (dreams, relationships between fathers and sons). Also when Luis Buñuel had the grandfather in *Diary of a Chambermaid* call all the servant girls by the same name, this was hailed as an original directorial strategy indicating the quality of the old man's social and sexual relationships. No critic recalled that the device had been used to precisely the same effect in a modest little Forties thriller, *Nocturne*.

Also, the Western and the gangster film have a special relationship with American society. Both deal with critical phases of American history. It could be said that they represent America talking to itself about, in the case of the Western, its agrarian past, and in the case of the gangster film/thriller, its urban technological present. To amplify and illustrate this, there is a fairly consistent attitude in Westerns to, for example, homesteading and the tillers of the soil. Where they are present they are almost invariably depicted sympathetically (e.g. *Shane*, the films of John Ford), sometimes with overtones of divine ordination (*The Covered Wagon*, *The Westerner*). This is a modern restatement of a traditional attitude to the West and to the frontier farmer in American culture. Its growth is traced historically by Henry Nash Smith in his *Virgin Land: the American West as Symbol and Myth*:

With each surge of westward movement a new community came into being. These communities devoted themselves not to marching onward but to cultivating the earth. They plowed the virgin land and put in crops, and the great Interior Valley was transformed into a garden: for the imagination, the Garden of the World. The image of this vast and constantly growing agricultural society in the interior of the continent became one of the dominant symbols of nineteenth century American society – a collective representation, a poetic idea (as Tocqueville noted in the early 1830s) that defined the promise of American life. The master symbol of the garden embraced a cluster of metaphors expressing fecundity, growth, increase and blissful labor in the earth, all centring about the heroic figure of the idealized frontier farmer with that supreme agrarian weapon, the sacred plow.

Conversely, the Western incorporates sometimes ambivalent attitudes to industrialisation, usually manifested as gold or silver-mining and the railroad. Thus Ford and de Mille, in *The Iron Horse* and *Union Pacific*, explicitly celebrate the building of the transcontinental railways, but each shows that the railroad brought to the West a collection of whores, gamblers, land

18

speculators and assorted con-men. The principal symbol of this anti-industrialism in the Western is mining, as in *The Far Country*, *Bend of the River* and *Guns in the Afternoon*. These are only two of the many, sometimes contradictory, attitudes found in the Western, which may also of course accommodate responses to contemporary events. Thus *Broken Arrow* was among the first of many Westerns to make reference to race prejudice, while *High Noon* and *Johnny Guitar* were, in some senses, reactions to McCarthyism.

There has been a curious reluctance among film critics to confront the notion of genre, the most usual reason offered being that genres are collections of neutral conventions which the director either animates or not, according to his qualities as author. If he is Nicholas Ray, he transcends the genre; if he is Edward Dmytryk, he makes just another Western. This position seems at odds with the importance placed on genre by both film-makers and audiences. Several film-makers, for instance Howard Hawks and Richard Brooks, have taken conscious decisions to make Westerns at particular points in their careers, and there is good evidence for believing that on the whole the most coherent and personal work of Ford, Mann and Boetticher has been within that genre. In addition, audiences seem to know exactly what they are getting from a Western or a gangster film even if they do not make this knowledge articulate. The responses of film-makers and audiences to the genres seem to offer a good *prima facie* case for believing that they are animating rather than neutral, that they carry intrinsic charges of meaning independently of whatever is brought to them by particular directors. To make a guess, it would seem possible that while the film-maker may respond primarily to the genres' archetypal qualities, the audience responds to their historical qualities. To put it another way, our response to the Western may be coloured by our response to the epic quality of the opening of the West, to the gangster film by our response to the violence and excitement of American cities, especially in the Prohibition period. To complete the circle, our ideas about

19

both these historical phenomena are very likely gleaned primarily from the cinema.

Resistance to the idea of the usefulness of genre as an element in critical debate has come from two quarters. Critics practising an unrefined application of the *auteur* theory are deflected from paying particular attention to genre by the internal logic of their critical method. If the purpose of the method is to reveal the hand of a director (or possibly, writer) in a number of films, then other considerations naturally recede. The second area of resistance to the idea of the animating power of genre is, surprisingly, among some of those seeking a general semiology of the cinema. Surprisingly, because genre, with its obvious analogies with a sign system, an agreed code between film-maker and audience, would seem on the face of it a fruitful starting-point for investigating the semiology of the cinema.

The best writers on the Western, Bazin, Wagner, Rieupeyrout and Lovell, all discuss the form primarily in thematic terms. Thus Alan Lovell, talking about the elements that came together to make the classical Western, names the plot elements of hero, heroine, villain and action in early Westerns, the epic theme as in *The Covered Wagon*, and the revenge theme as in *My Darling Clementine*. Similarly, the best writing about the gangster film/thriller, like Borde and Chaumeton's *Panorama du Film Noir Américain*, is expressed primarily in thematic terms. Even if it displays great sensitivity to the formal properties of the genre, as does Robert Warshow's *The Gangster as Tragic Hero*, ultimately it is more concerned with socio-cultural than formal questions. Is there an alternative method of writing about genre which will bring it more clearly within the province of semiology? The answer to this question would seem to lie in the nature of the relationship between genre and audience, in the fact that the audience seems to assimilate genre cinema with ease and has a set of expectations in relation to it.

A possible historical analogy is with the relationship between medieval and renaissance man and his art. It seems certain that an ordinary Frenchman of the thirteenth century could 'read' Chartres Cathedral and that a seventeenth century Venetian could 'read' Francesco Maffei's painting of Judith of Bethulia which, according to Erwin Panofsky, we would be liable to confuse with contemporary paintings of Salome. In both cases the contemporary audience understood the iconography of the works in question, the meaning within their cultures of the objects depicted. It would seem appropriate to recall Christian Metz's suggestion that one of the two valid areas of study for the semiologist of the cinema is iconography, and to point out that the example he quotes from Rieupeyrout, good and bad cowboys in white and black shirts respectively, is from genre cinema. To describe its iconography would seem, therefore, the most convenient starting-place for a description of the gangster film/thriller.

The automobile as murder weapon: Frank Sinatra in *Tony Rome*; Marlon Brando and Eva Marie Saint in *On the Waterfront*

22

# 2: Iconography

In *Little Caesar* (1930) a police lieutenant and two of his men visit a night-club run by gangsters. All three wear large hats and heavy coats, are grim and sardonic and stand in triangular formation, the lieutenant at the front, his two men flanking him in the rear. The audience knows immediately what to expect of them by their physical attributes, their dress and deportment. It knows, too, by the disposition of the figures, which is dominant, which subordinate. In *The Harder They Fall* (1956) a racketeer and two of his men go to a rendezvous in downtown New York. As they wait for the door of the building to be opened they take up the same formation as the figures in the earlier film, giving the same information to the audience by the same means. (The fact that they are, in the first case, policemen, and in the second case, racketeers, is an interesting ambiguity which will be examined later.) In *On the Waterfront* (1954) and in *Tony Rome* (1967) there are carefully mounted scenes in which the central figure is walking down a dark and deserted street. In each case an automobile drives swiftly towards him; and the audience, drawing on accumulated experiences of the genre, realises that it will be used as a murder weapon against the hero. Both these examples indicate the continuity over several decades of patterns of visual imagery, of recurrent objects and figures in dynamic relationship. These repeated patterns might be called the iconography of the genre, for they set it off visually from other types of film and are the means whereby primary definitions are made.

The recurrent patterns of imagery can be usefully divided into three categories: those surrounding the physical presence, attributes and dress of the actors and the characters they play; those emanating from the milieux within which the characters operate; and those connected with the technology at the characters' disposal. Among Hollywood leading men, Edward G. Robinson and James Cagney dominate the gangster films of the Thirties; Humphrey Bogart the thrillers and Richard Widmark the gangster films of the Forties; and, though not in such a clear-cut way, Richard Conte has a good claim to this role in the gangster films of the Fifties. In addition to these major icons of the genres, there are other players of the second rank such as George Bancroft, Barton Maclane, Joe Sawyer, Paul Kelly, Bob Steele, Ted de Corsia, Charles McGraw and Jack Lambert, to name only a few, who have become inseparably associated with the gangster film/thriller. The American cinema has traditionally achieved its effects with the utmost directness, and never more so than in the casting of gangster films and thrillers. Men such as Cagney, Robinson and Bogart seem to gather within themselves the qualities of the genres they appear in so that the violence, suffering and *angst* of the films is restated in their faces, physical presence, movement and speech. By the curious alchemy of the cinema, each successive appearance in the genre further solidifies the actor's screen persona until he no longer plays a role but assimilates it to the collective entity made up of his own body and personality and his past screen roles. For instance, the beat-up face, tired eyes and rasping voice by which we identify Humphrey Bogart are, in part, selections we have made from his roles as Sam Spade, Philip Marlowe and others.

It is not only the actors playing the roles who recur, but the roles themselves. Genres become definable as such by repetition until fairly fixed conventions are established, and this is particularly apparent in the spectrum of characters in the

24

gangster film/thriller: racketeers with brains who rise to the top, gangsters without who remain as hoods, gangsters' women, stool pigeons, cops and bent cops, crusading district attorneys and legal mouthpieces for the mobs, private eyes and heroes forced by circumstances to be such, night-club owners and their sadistic strong-arm men; and the countless secondary figures on the fringes of this dark world, newspapermen, poolroom and gymnasium owners, newsvendors and so on. The interpretation of these roles may develop. For instance, James Cagney's particular physical dynamism was interpreted, in the gangster films of the Thirties, as necessary ruthlessness in getting to the top, but in the gangster films he made in the post-war period, especially *White Heat* (1949) and *Kiss Tomorrow Goodbye* (1951), this physical dynamism was interpreted as psychotic. A touchstone of normality is usually present, often centred on the figure of the gangster's mother. This is apparent in the earliest examples of the genre such as *Little Caesar* (1930), *The Public Enemy* (1931) and *Scarface* (1932); it is present vestigially in *The Big Heat* (1954) and achieves almost pristine restatement in *The Brothers Rico* (1957).

But the figures in the gangster film/thriller proclaim themselves not only by their physical attributes and their roles but also by their dress. The peculiar squareness of their hatted and coated figures is an extension of their physical presence, a visual shorthand for their violent potential. Clothes have always been important in the gangster film, not only as carriers of iconographic meaning but also as objects which mark the gangster's increasing status. Scenes in tailors' shops are frequent (*The Public Enemy*; *Al Capone* (1959)), and both Rico (*Little Caesar*) and Tony Camonte (*Scarface*) invite comments on their clothes ('How do you like it? Expensive, huh?'). Alec Styles, the gangleader in *The Street With No Name* (1948), tells a new member of his gang, 'Buy yourself a closetful of clothes. I like my boys to look sharp.' Characters in *Baby Face Nelson* (1957) ('Get rid of that gunny-sack') and *Murder Inc.* (1951) ('Burn that tent you're wearing') are instructed to

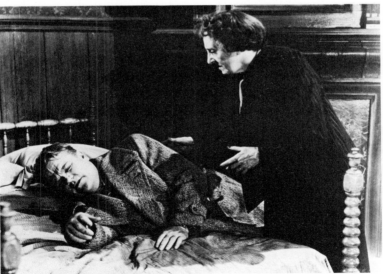

Inflections on the figure of the gangster's mother: (*above*) Alexander Scourby and portrait in *The Big Heat*; (*below*) James Cagney, Margaret Wycherly in *White Heat*

change their clothes as a mark of their rising status, and Tolly Devlin's ascent within the syndicate in *Underworld USA* (1960) is marked by syndicate boss Gela's comments on his clothes.

Following *The Naked City* (1948), several gangster films and thrillers appeared carrying the word 'city' in their titles: *Dark City, Cry of the City, City Across the River, While the City Sleeps, The Sleeping City, Captive City* and so on. Alongside these came other films featuring the word 'street' in their titles: *The Street With No Name, Race Street, Side Street, Down Three Dark Streets, The Naked Street,* not to mention *Where the Sidewalk Ends* and *The Asphalt Jungle.* This development simply made explicit what had always been an important element of the gangster film/thriller, the urban milieu.* Robert Warshow, in his essay *The Gangster As Tragic Hero,* writes:

The gangster is the man of the city, with the city's language and knowledge, with its queer and dishonest skills and its terrible daring, carrying his life in his hands like a placard, like a club ... for the gangster there is only the city; he must inhabit it in order to personify it: not the real city, but that dangerous and sad city of the imagination which is so much more important, which is the modern world.

Thus the city milieu serves both as a background for the activities of the gangster and the hero of the thriller, and as a kind of expressionist extension of the violence and brutality of their world. The sub-milieux of the gangster film/thriller are, in fact,

---

* There is within the gangster film a sub-genre beginning with *Dillinger* (1945) and culminating in *Bonnie and Clyde* (1967) in which the action does not take place in the city, but in the small towns of the rural mid-West. Even within the gangster films of the Thirties [*G-Men* (1935) for instance] the conventions allowed the city milieu to be forsaken for a final shoot-up at the gansters' mountain hideout. Thrillers of the last decade have tended to move from the city to more exotic locales such as Florida and the Californian coast.

'The dangerous, sad city of the imagination': *He Walked by Night*

recurrent selections from real city locales: dark streets, dingy rooming-houses and office blocks, bars, night-clubs, penthouse apartments, precinct stations and, especially in the thriller, luxurious mansions. These milieux, charged with the tension of the violence and mystery enacted within them, are most often seen at night, lit by feeble street lights or more garish neon signs, such as the Cook's Tours sign 'The World is Yours' in *Scarface*, or the flickering signs which cast threatening shadows and half-disclose mysterious visitors in the offices of Sam Spade (*The Maltese Falcon*) and Philip Marlowe (*Farewell, My Lovely*). Fritz Lang, in his German film *Metropolis*, created a huge city embodying his expressionist fantasies. When he came to America he had no need to re-create his city; it already existed.

The gangster and the hero of the thriller, being modern men of the city, have at their disposal the city's complex technology, in particular the firearms, automobiles and telephones which are recurrent images of the genre. It is fitting that the Western hero, moving balletically through his archaic world, should bear graceful weapons such as the Winchester rifle and the Colt pistol. The weaponry of the gangster film/thriller is much more squat and ugly: the police ·38, which forms the title image of *Kiss of Death* and the opening image of *The Big Heat*; the Luger; the sawn-off shotgun; the sub-machine-gun which becomes an object of veneration in *Scarface* and *Machine-Gun Kelly*. Andrew Sinclair, in his book *Prohibition: the Era of Excess*, describes the role of the automobile in the Prohibition/repeal debate:

The armour-plated cars with windows of bullet-proof glass, the murders implicit in Hymie Weiss's phrase 'to take for a ride', the sedans of tommy-gunners spraying the streets of gangland, all created a satanic mythology of the automobile which bid fair to rival the demonism of the saloon. The car was an instrument of death in the hands of the crook and drunk, and prohibition was held to have spawned both of them.

The automobile is a major icon in the gangster film/thriller. It has a twofold function in the gangster film: it is the means whereby the hero carries out his 'work' (Tom and Eddie in *The Public Enemy*, waiting orders from Nails Nathan, stand beside their car like the crew of a Panzer about to go into action); and it becomes, like his clothes, the visible token of his success. Eventually it becomes the symbol of his unbridled aggressiveness, and it seems perfectly logical that the automobile should be used regularly as a lethal instrument in both thrillers and gangster films (see *The Dark Corner*, *Underworld USA*, *The Moving Target* and others).* So powerful a symbol has it become of the gangster's presence that characters may respond

---

* The menace of the automobile is not, of course, confined to the gangster film and thriller. Cars are used as blunt instruments in, for example, the black comedy *It's a Mad, Mad, Mad, Mad World*.

Clothes and cars as marks of rising status: Edward Woods and James Cagney in *The Public Enemy*

with fear to an automobile without seeing the men within it (see *Kiss of Death*, *The Garment Jungle*, *Assignment to Kill* and others).

The telephone has, on occasion, been used as a murder weapon in the gangster film/thriller and this, too, seems logical. The physical environment, an expressionist representation of the violent potential in the genres, becomes the instrument of violence. More often, however, telephones are used to intimidate the weak, as in the threatening calls to Mrs Renato in *The Garment Jungle* and to Mrs Bannion in *The Big Heat*.

It is, of course, an artificial exercise to discuss individual iconographic elements when they exist in dynamic relationship within the fabric of particular films. Now and then several iconographical elements combine in singular purity and there are found the sequences most characteristic of the genres. For instance, the opening sequence of *The Harder They Fall*, showing several figures (Bogart, racketeers and others) entering cars and hurtling through the empty New York streets to an early morning rendezvous, evokes brilliantly the ugliness of the milieu and the ruthlessness of the racketeers before disclosing the squalid operation they are embarked upon. Again, the sequence in *Little Caesar* when Tony, the gang's driver, is shot down on the steps of the church by Rico from a speeding car, brings dynamically together several iconographical elements. The same elements are interestingly used in the French gangster film *Le Deuxième Souffle*, in which the trademark of the central figure is to shoot his victims inside a car which he himself drives. Perhaps the iconography of the gangster film is presented most strikingly (and, incidentally, the non-realistic quality of the genre most clearly exemplified) in the characteristic montage sequences of Thirties gangster films where the outbreak of gang war is chronicled. The films at these points prise themselves free from their inhibiting narrative structures and present the pure imagery of aggression: speeding cars, screaming tyres, figures blasting each other with revolvers and sub-machine-guns. A frozen frame from such a sequence would

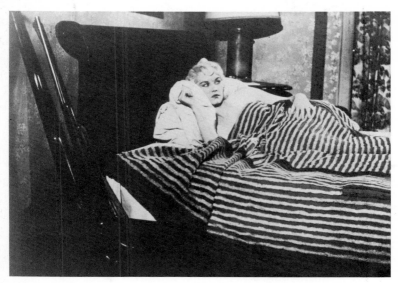

Violence and sexuality: Dorothy Provine in *The Bonnie Parker Story*

look like a pop art poster representation of the essence of the gangster film.

But to define the gangster film/thriller solely by its iconography is to suggest that the genre is static and unchanging, that the gangster film of the Thirties is indistinguishable from that of the Fifties, or the Forties thriller from its counterpart of the Sixties. In fact, both thrillers and gangster films, especially the latter, are in constant flux, adding a new thematic dimension here, a new moral emphasis there.

# 3: Development

The first phase of the gangster film began in 1930 with Mervyn LeRoy's *Little Caesar*. The genre reached a point of classical development unusually soon after its appearance, and fully developed examples – William Wellman's *The Public Enemy* (1931) and Howard Hawks' *Scarface* (1932) – are very close, iconographically and thematically, to *Little Caesar*. This phase went into decline in the year that *Scarface* was produced, as is indicated by the baroque variations of Wellman's *The Hatchet Man* (1932), in which the themes and conventions of the classical gangster film are played out, somewhat bizarrely, in San Francisco's Chinatown.

There had, of course, been crime films before *Little Caesar*, but they cannot, iconographically or thematically, be called gangster films. This is best illustrated by comparing *Little Caesar* with a crime film of the silent period, Josef von Sternberg's *Underworld* (1927). The latter makes no reference to Prohibition; the central criminal figure, Bull Weed, seems to derive his income from snatching jewels; he is not surrounded by the deferential hoods of the gangster film, but has informal contacts with a series of shady characters in bowler hats and striped jerseys reminiscent of the underworld of *The Threepenny Opera*; the iconography of guns, automobiles and telephones is scarcely apparent; and the film is principally concerned (apart from its obvious formal preoccupations) with the triangular relationship involving Bull Weed, his girl, and an alcoholic Englishman. Only in the final shoot-up does *Underworld* begin to look like a gangster film, and this bears a marked resemblance to the ending of *Scarface*, very likely explicable by the fact that Ben Hecht wrote both films. A comparison between the two endings illustrates the importance of sound in the gangster genre. In *Scarface* the audience *hears* the exploding tear gas shells and the bullets from the police machine-guns; in *Underworld* it merely sees them.

*Little Caesar*, on the other hand, carries most of the iconographical features of the genre: guns, automobiles, the presence of Edward G. Robinson, square figures disposed in formation, and so on; and it displays the same central thematic concerns as *The Public Enemy* and *Scarface*. Each film examines the precipitate rise and fall of a gangster: Rico in *Little Caesar*, Tom Powers in *The Public Enemy*, and Tony Camonte in *Scarface*. All three are from immigrant Catholic backgrounds; they are expansive, vulgar and garrulous, and in their compulsive drive for success seem like criminal disciples of Horatio Alger. Their methods are summed up in Tony Camonte's advice to his friend Guino Rinaldo, 'Do it first, do it yourself, and keep on doing it.' Their sexual relationships are abnormal: Rico eschews women and there is a strong suggestion of homosexual involvement with his dancer friend; Tony Camonte has an incestuous relationship with his sister; and Tom Powers' attitude to women is so dominating as to seem aberrant. Camonte and Powers earn their living by peddling illicit liquor, but so completely do the films concentrate on the violence of their activities – killing rival gangsters, or fellow mobsters who block their rise to power – that they seem undifferentiated from Rico, who gets his money by robbery. They all die in a similar manner: Tom Powers trussed like a mummy and dumped on his mother's doorstep, Rico and Camonte machine-gunned in the street. That the gangster must ultimately lie dead in the street became perhaps the most rigid convention of the genre, repeated through successive phases of its

35

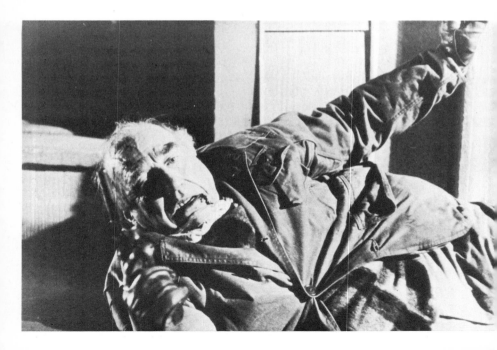

development (see *The Roaring Twenties, Dillinger, Cry of the City, Party Girl, The Lineup, New York Confidential, The Naked Street, The Rise and Fall of Legs Diamond, Underworld USA* and others) and extending into European cinema through films like *A Bout de Souffle.*

Even as the classic gangster films of the first phase were going into decline, forces were gathering to hasten their demise. Films such as *Little Caesar* and *Scarface* and the sixty or so others produced in the period were constructed so unambiguously round the gangster as hero that the genre became a major battleground in the growing pressure for censorship of the movies. Both *The Public Enemy* and *Scarface* carry hastily added denunciatory prologues against the gangster, and the latter includes some lame scenes of newspaper editors fulminating and bourgeois citizens organising against crime. The movement towards censorship of the American cinema achieved its most solid statement in the formation in 1934 of the Legion of Decency; but by this time the first phase of the genre was dead.

The second phase emerged in 1935 with William Keighley's *G-Men*. Like the cycle of similar films which followed it in the next three years, *G-Men* was iconographically indistinguishable from the gangster films of the first phase, but it had an F.B.I. agent as the central figure. This appeased the censors, though the behaviour of the G-men (James Cagney played the lead) was no different from that of the gangsters they supplanted. The obvious problem for the film-makers of the period was to give the G-men's antagonists, the gangsters, some independent life, some identity. This was done by involving the G-man hero on a personal basis with the mob, usually by having him join it in order to destroy it, a device which recurs not only in this phase of the genre's development but also in succeeding, post-war phases (see *The Street With No Name* and *Underworld USA*). The G-man hero was quickly joined by the policeman hero. William Keighley's *Bullets or Ballots* (1936) uses the pretence that the policeman (Edward G. Robinson) has been dismissed from the force so that he can join and destroy

◀ 'That the gangster must ultimately lie dead in the street became perhaps the most rigid convention of the genre': (*left*) *Baby Face Nelson* and *Odds Against Tomorrow*, (*right*) *Side Street* and *The Roaring Twenties*

the gang. Soon there was added the figure of the Special Prosecutor, a lawyer given dictatorial powers to clean up a city (see Lloyd Bacon's *Racket Busters* (1938)).

Up to this point in its development, the explicit attitude of the gangster film to the criminal had been a simple one. Criminals are born, not made; they are incapable of reform and can be stopped only by being destroyed. It is true that *The Public Enemy*, in the scenes in which young Tom and Matt graduate from petty crime to grand larceny and violence, has the materials for a statement about the social origins of crime, but this is not developed. The possibility of such a statement does not reappear until William Wyler's *Dead End* (1937), marking the beginning of the next phase of the genre.

Films such as *Crime School*, *Gangster's Boy*, *Angels With Dirty Faces*, all made in 1938, and the other films of this cycle, show an awareness that bad home conditions, a criminal environment, and the brutal treatment of young people in reform schools, produce criminals. But again, especially in *Angels With Dirty Faces*, the gangster is at the emotional centre of most of these films. There is, too, a particular device, first used in *Angels With Dirty Faces* and later to become important in post-war phases of the genre, which seems to undercut any statement about the social origins of crime which the films purport to make. This device is to have the gangster and one of the establishment figures in the film (priest, policeman, lawyer) come from the same slum neighbourhood, suggesting, but seldom in the pre-war period at least making explicit, that the badness of the one and the goodness of the other are the result of moral choice rather than social conditioning.

Although successive phases of the genre are discernible and their emergence can be dated, gangster films with many of the features of earlier phases continued to be made, so that in the period 1938–39, for example, one can find films like *When G-Men Step In*, an example of the G-man cycle, *I Am the Law*, which uses the device of the Special Prosecutor, *Angels Wash Their Faces*, a film with an ostensibly social theory of crime,

Gangster and Establishment figure from the same slum neighbourhood: James Cagney and Pat O'Brien in *Angels With Dirty Faces*

and *The Roaring Twenties* which, with certain qualifications, could have been made at any time in the decade. However, the notion that criminals are formed by social conditioning, and are therefore capable of reform, was in the air, as is evident by the way it seeps into the least likely films, including the more traditional kinds of gangster film. Fritz Lang, in *You Only Live Once* (1937), presents the criminal as demonstrably capable of reform, but thwarted by social and even metaphysical forces quite beyond his control; in *You and Me* (1938), he examines the soulless mechanics of the parole system. *The Roaring Twenties* suggests that the experience of violence in the First World War, and the bitterness of unemployment after it, forced men into crime; both *The Roaring Twenties* and *The Big Shot* (1942) have secondary heroes, young men on the fringes of the criminal world represented by the gangsters around whom the films revolve. But the more traditional iconographical elements survive. *The Big Shot* has probably the most exciting car chase in the genre, along the snow-covered roads of New York State. And the thematic preoccupation with the success and downfall of the gangster survives also. 'Who is he?' asks a policeman over the figure lying dead in the street at the end of *The Roaring Twenties*. 'Eddie Bartlett; he used to be a big shot,' replies the dead man's ex-partner. Duke Berne, dying in the prison hospital at the end of *The Big Shot*, laughs with bitter self-accusation, 'Knew all the angles; big shot!'

The gangster genre at the end of the Thirties thus survived with several encrustations: the G-man/policeman/Special Prosecutor hero, and an ostensibly social theory of crime. There occurred, however, in 1941 a development in the genre so radical as to seem almost a metamorphosis. John Huston's *The Maltese Falcon* marks the break with the preoccupations of the Thirties, yet it continues the tradition going back to *Little Caesar* in two ways. Iconographically it is closely linked to the gangster film: the action is played out in urban milieux of dark streets, seedy office blocks and luxury hotel apartments; the technological icons, guns and telephones in this case, are evident; and the human icons, Humphrey Bogart, Barton Maclane and others, are, in dress and deportment, conventional figures of the gangster movie. The central figure is a private investigator, a familiar figure in the American cinema of the Thirties (The Thin Man, Nero Wolfe, Charlie Chan, Ellery Queen, Mr Moto, the Lone Wolf), if somewhat outside the mainstream of the gangster film. But *The Maltese Falcon* is set radically apart from the crime films of the Thirties by its sense of human isolation and its awareness of evil. *The Maltese Falcon* is discussed in some detail in a subsequent chapter. The archetypal elements of the thriller can be illustrated here, however, by looking at Howard Hawks' version of Raymond Chandler's *The Big Sleep* (1946).

Its hero Philip Marlowe (Humphrey Bogart), a hard-bitten, ageing private investigator, is summoned to the luxurious mansion of General Sternwood and asked to deal with the man holding the gambling debts of the General's younger daughter, Carmen. Marlowe's investigations lead him into a fragmented and incomprehensible world peopled by characters whose motivation, commitment, and sometimes precise identity, are unclear. Where is Sean Regan, what is the nature of Vivian's relationship with Eddie Mars, what is Mars' connection with the blackmailer Geiger, who is Harry Jones, the little man tailing Marlowe, where does Mona Mars' loyalty lie? The fluidity of allegiances is best exemplified in Agnes' serving Geiger, Brody and Harry Jones in turn, and – archetypally in the genre – in whether the central female figure, in this case Vivian Sternwood (Lauren Bacall), will prove true or false to the hero. The identity of Marlowe himself dissolves into several personae he adopts: as a collector of rare books, as a policeman (to get Agnes' address), as a passing motorist (to gain access to Mona Mars' house). In the complex patterns of seeming and being in the genre, even objects withhold their true meanings: the head of a Buddha conceals a camera, Geiger's diary is in code, a drink offered as whisky contains cyanide. The clouding of the characters' motivations and identities is reflected in the exterior physical environment of the film: darkness, mist and torrential rain.

The veiled reactions of the characters sometimes give way to sudden outbursts of violence, as in the shooting of Geiger, Brody and Mars, and the beating up of Marlowe, first by anonymous hoods in the street, and later by Canino. Typically of the genre, the violence, its threat or aftermath, is often associated with automobiles: the Sternwood Packard is pulled from the sea bearing the murdered corpse of the chauffeur, Marlowe's car is used as an armoury, and it figures largely in the scene of Canino's death. In the opening scenes of the film, General Sternwood speaks of his orchids 'smelling of corruption' and of his daughter's 'corrupt blood'. The explicit imagery of this dialogue is implicit in the mood of the film thereafter, a mood often conveyed by hints of aberrant sexuality: the nymphomania of Carmen, the homosexual involvement of General

'. . . even objects withhold their true meanings': Humphrey Bogart in *The Big Sleep*

Sternwood with Sean Regan and of Geiger with Carol Lundgren, the pornographic photographs taken by Geiger. Also typical of the genre, an attachment to art is an index of corruption: Geiger is a collector of rare books and his house is decorated with oriental artefacts.

As applied to films like *The Maltese Falcon, The Big Sleep* and other private-eye movies of the Forties, the label thriller is perhaps less satisfactory than the French critical term *film noir*, which comments on the mood of the films; though since it comments on a mood rather than on a set of conventions making up a genre, it can be applied to individual films, thrillers, gangster films, police documentaries, or even to films in which the crime element is marginal, such as *Lost Weekend*. However, since the *noir* element is so strikingly present during the period, it is a very useful term for discussing American cinema of the Forties. Black thrillers in the style of *The Maltese Falcon* do not emerge fully as a genre until the immediate post-war period, but the mood is increasingly apparent in crime films of the war years.

The American cinema had always sought in its players physical presence or gestures which could convey states of mind or character. And in the *film noir* the physical qualities of the villains are used as visual shorthand to suggest depths of evil. Hence obesity – Sydney Greenstreet in *The Maltese Falcon* and Laird Cregar in *Hot Spot* (1942) – and hence the sinister, babyish Peter Lorre, and Elisha Cook's tormented eyes. In *This Gun for Hire*, paradoxically, the device is used in reverse: Alan Ladd's sculptured beauty becomes a visual shorthand for psychosis. Probably the same impulse, together with Hollywood's anti-intellectualism, often caused the evil of villains in the *film noir* to be exteriorised in the form of a commitment to art. This is usually presented as the acquisitiveness of the collector or critic, as in *The Maltese Falcon, The Big Sleep, Laura, The Dark Corner* (Clifton Webb figures archetypally in this role), rather than as the creativity of the artist, as in *The Phantom Lady*.

44

(*left*) Art and evil: Clifton Webb in *Laura*; (*right*) art and violence: Pat O'Brien in *Crackup*

The five years between the end of the Second World War and the close of the Forties saw several concurrent developments: the black thriller was established, the gangster film re-emerged in new forms, and a new sub-genre, the semi-documentary, appeared. While these developments are virtually simultaneous and, in certain manifestations, separable, they are interpenetrated to a remarkable degree, and almost all show, in one way or another, the influence of the *film noir*. Indeed, it is possible to discuss the development of the *film noir* by reference to films in all these categories.

The morally equivocal hero of the thriller regularly receives at his office callers who invite him to recover valuable objects or missing persons (*Farewell, My Lovely*), and sometimes, inexplicably, menace him (*The Dark Corner*). Like a figure in a paranoid nightmare, he is persecuted and offered violence to dissuade him from further investigation, and often he finds those who have assisted him murdered (*The Big Sleep, Dead Reckoning*). Most uncertain of all is the commitment of the central female figure, who may prove true to him (*The Big Sleep, Dark Passage*) or false (*Dead Reckoning*), but who will almost certainly sexually enslave him. This somewhat misogynist element of the *film noir* finds its way into gangster films of the time (*The Killers, Criss Cross*) and into films concerned with domestic crime (*Double Indemnity*). The Circe figure quite often entices the hero by her song (*Dead Reckoning, The Killers*), or by her dance (*Criss Cross*), and she is usually played by actresses of startlingly sensual unreality (Lauren Bacall, Lizabeth Scott, Barbara Stanwyck). The dissembled passion of the *femme fatale* is characteristic of the *film noir*, but there are also other forms of sexual interest: the hopeless love of an old man for a young woman (*Farewell, My Lovely, The Dark Corner*), nymphomania (*The Big Sleep*), homosexuality (*The Big Sleep, Farewell, My Lovely*) and frigidity (*The High Window*).

The cruelty of the *film noir* is as evident in the thrillers as in the gangster films of the period. Although there are numerous killings in the gangster films of the Thirties, the attendant violence is swift, usually occasioned by gunfire and quite un-ritualised. The *film noir* ritualised and refined violence. Victims are dispatched by poison (*The Big Sleep*), defenestration (*The Dark Corner*), and a steam-hammer (*Brute Force*) into which the victim is driven by lighted blow-torches. Although about prison life, *Brute Force* bears many of the marks of the *film noir*, including a sadistic prison officer, conceived in Nietzschean terms, who plays Wagner on the gramophone while beating up a prisoner. Several villains are presented as sadists (*Dead Reckoning, Kiss of Death*) and almost all have unusual physical characteristics. Bob Steele, who plays Canino in *The Big Sleep*, has the coldest eyes in cinema; and Richard Widmark's laugh so unnervingly evoked the psychosis of the character he plays in *Kiss of Death* that he has seldom laughed again on the screen.

46

'Like a figure in a paranoid nightmare . . .': James Garner in *Marlowe*

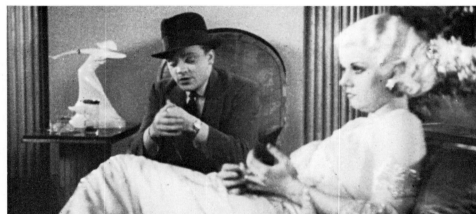

The gangster film re-emerged in two forms in the post-war period. *Dillinger* (1945) forsook the urban milieu and the immigrant Catholic racketeer. Its central figure, John Dillinger, of American Protestant stock, a product of the Depression, operated as a bank robber in the semi-rural mid-West. This type of gangster film was not extensively produced at this time (one of the few examples is the infinitely more accomplished *They Live by Night* of Nicholas Ray), but it reappeared in the mid-Fifties and again in the mid-Sixties. A far more interesting type of gangster film is that represented by *Kiss of Death* (1947) and *Force of Evil* (1949), both of which are concerned with the relationship of one man to the world of crime. In each case the hero has to make a moral decision about what that relationship is to be. *Force of Evil*, Abraham Polonsky's first film as director, is especially interesting. In addition to presenting the moral dilemma facing the hero, the film equates crime with capitalistic enterprise and reaches out towards a more general statement about man's inclination towards evil.

The greatest amount of critical attention in this period was accorded to a group of films known variously as 'semi-documentaries' and 'police documentaries'. Their appearance is usually associated with the name of the *March of Time* producer Louis de Rochemont, who, possibly influenced by Italian neo-realism, persuaded Darryl Zanuck to allow him to use documentary techniques on feature films. The first such film, *The House on 92nd Street* (1945), dealt with the FBI's unmasking of a German spy-ring in the United States. It carries most of the marks of this sub-genre: an announcement that the material is factual, shooting on actual locations, the use, where possible, of people actually involved in the events depicted, and careful documentation of FBI processes such as filing, operating concealed cameras, editing and viewing film of espionage activities. It is a measure of the interpenetration of moods, techniques and attitudes of the time that the techniques of the semi-documentary are apparent in a thriller such as *Dark Passage* and a gangster film such as *Kiss of Death*, while

49

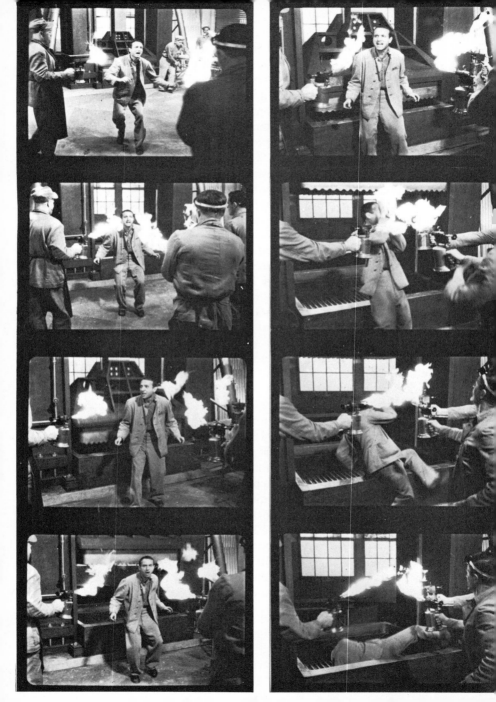

one of the best examples of the sub-genre, *Boomerang* (1947), deals with the same moral dilemma as the gangster film *Force of Evil*. While it is an interesting critical exercise to isolate these impulses, ultimately they exist woven together in the fabric of particular films.

The thriller, the morally oriented gangster film and the semi-documentary are therefore the hallmarks of the Forties; but a coda was added to the decade by the appearance of a handful of films constructed round the dynamic presence of James Cagney. Of these the most striking are *White Heat* (1949) and, to a lesser extent, *Kiss Tomorrow Goodbye* (1951). As in the Thirties, he is at the emotional centre of these gangster films, but they bear the marks of their time in that the mobsters live by robbery rather than by Prohibition racketeering, and both films show the influence of the *film noir* and the semi-documentary. The Cagney character in *White Heat* has the most explicit Oedipus complex in cinema. The extreme violence in the film is of its time (for example, the disfigurement of a man by scalding steam), and characteristic also is the way in which the police, in detecting the gang, make use of a battery of communications devices. *Kiss Tomorrow Goodbye* is remarkable for its picture of unrelieved corruption in official circles (prison guards, police, lawyers), and again for the characteristic quality of its violence.

The thriller survives into the Fifties, when it is dominated by adaptations from the novels of Mickey Spillane: *I, the Jury* (1953), *Kiss Me Deadly* (1955), *My Gun is Quick* (1958). The private investigator hero of these films, considerably nastier than his counterpart in the Forties, is perhaps best rendered in the mesomorphic presence of Ralph Meeker in *Kiss Me Deadly*, in which the hero intimidates innocent people to get information. A particular feature of these films is the procession of women who cross the hero's path and whom he uses with icy detachment (in this sense these films are progenitors of the James Bond cycle). The semi-documentary progressively

51

withered in the Fifties, but the morally oriented gangster film still presents the hero with the dilemma of moral choice in *On the Waterfront* (1954) and *The Garment Jungle* (1957), both, incidentally, about labour racketeering. Several of the gangster films of the late Forties, in addition to being influenced by the *film noir* and the semi-documentary, had involved the careful planning and execution of a large-scale robbery (*Criss Cross, White Heat*), which nevertheless remained secondary to the examination of character and obsession and the evocation of mood in these films. *The Asphalt Jungle* (1950) was unique in the attention it gave to the mechanics of planning and executing the robbery. It became the prototype of a series of films throughout the Fifties in which a group of men from various backgrounds, some criminal, some nearly so, some respectable, but all with special skills, come together for the purpose of the robbery, the rewards of which they are kept from enjoying by internal tensions and, sometimes, a malicious fate. The most distinguished of these is Stanley Kubrick's *The Killing* (1956), but the same impulse is apparent in *Seven Thieves* (1960) and *Odds Against Tomorrow* (1959). The cycle survived into the Sixties. Notable foreign versions of the theme include Jules Dassin's *Rififi* (1955), Basil Dearden's *League of Gentlemen* (1960), Giuliano Montaldo's *Grand Slam* (1967) and Antonio Isasi's *They Came to Rob Las Vegas* (1968), the last being almost a summation of all gangster films in which technology is extensively deployed.

The gangster film which forms the watershed between the Forties and the Fifties is *Murder Inc.* (1951). It bears many of the marks of the semi-documentary film − based on actual events, location photography, emphasis on the mechanics of investigation, large numbers of unknown players − but it also sounds for the first time the dominant note of the Fifties gangster film, the existence of a nation-wide criminal organisa-tion. In the case of *Murder Inc.*, it is a national organisation dealing in murder, but in later films of the decade the organisa-tion, increasingly known as 'the syndicate', controls gambling,

53

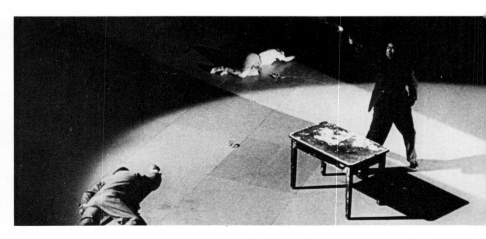

Chicago reconstructed: Richard Wilson's *Al Capone*

narcotics, labour racketeering and prostitution: *New York Confidential* (1954), *The Brothers Rico* (1957), *Underworld USA* (1960). There are several films in which the syndicate's operations are confined to a particular city – *The Big Heat* (1953), *Phoenix City Story* (1956) – but in most films of the type, the syndicate is smashed principally by the efforts of one man whose motive is usually revenge for the death of his kin (*The Big Heat, The Brothers Rico, Underworld USA*). Although the syndicate series of films seems to dominate the genre in the Fifties, it ran, in part, concurrently with another group of gangster films introduced by Don Siegel's *Baby Face Nelson* (1957). This group of films, mostly conceived as biographies of Prohibition and Depression criminals – *The Bonnie Parker Story* (1958), *Machine-Gun Kelly* (1958), *Al Capone* (1959), *The Rise and Fall of Legs Diamond* (1959) and others – offered a historical reconstruction of the Twenties and

Mickey Spillane on film. Anthony Quinn and Peggy Castle in *The Long Wait*

Thirties, though at the same time they remained very much at a distance from the characters they dealt with, as if they had become folk-heroes. This series continues into the Sixties with Richard Wilson's *Pay or Die* (1960), about the growth of the Mafia in late nineteenth-century New York, and Joseph Pevney's *Portrait of a Mobster* (1961), a biography of Dutch Schultz. There was a hiatus for some years and the series re-emerged very powerfully in Arthur Penn's *Bonnie and Clyde* (1967) and Roger Corman's *The St Valentine's Day Massacre* (1967) and *Bloody Mama* (1969).

This series of historical reconstructions overlaps with the re-emergence of the Forties thriller, first visible in Jack Smight's *The Moving Target* (1966) and later exemplified in *Gunn* (1967), *Tony Rome* (1967), *A New Face in Hell* (1967) and *Assignment to Kill* (1967). All these films are aware that they are working within the Forties thriller/*film noir* tradition, and that is their principal failing: the sour elements and the sexual aberrance are handled extremely heavily (*Gunn* excepted). The audience is no longer allowed to deduce from the hero's physical presence that he is world-weary, cynical, hard-bitten and poor: it must see him remove last night's coffee grounds from the wastepaper basket (*The Moving Target*) or earn a few dollars by acting as co-respondent in a divorce case (*A New Face in Hell*). These new thrillers, perhaps because they are in colour, have forsaken the urban milieu for more exotic locales (the Californian coast in *Gunn*, Florida in *Tony Rome*, Switzerland in *Assignment to Kill* and, intermittently, the Caribbean in *A New Face in Hell*). By thus forsaking the city they have lost an important element of their iconography and a dimension of their meaning. The relaxation of censorship in the intervening two decades has meant that, whereas John Huston suggested an infinity of moral corruption by his hints of homosexuality in *The Maltese Falcon*, Gordon Douglas and John Guillermin play male and female homosexuality for laughs in the coarsest possible manner in *Tony Rome* and *A New Face in Hell*. Only in Blake Edwards' *Gunn* is the sexual

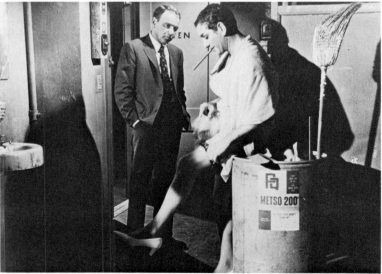

Explicit sexual aberration in the Sixties thriller: Frank Sinatra in *Tony Rome* and (*below*) *Lady in Cement*

57

Objective correlatives of evil: hoods in *The High Window*

aberration (the villain is a transvestite) a dimension of evil. Apart from *Gunn*, the most delicate and successful of these films is Buzz Kulik's *Warning Shot* (1966), which brilliantly exploits David Janssen's association with paranoia accumulated in his television series *The Fugitive*. With the utmost restraint, this film comes close to the sour mood of contemporary society.

# 4: Background

The gangster film and thriller have developed very strong conventions in their presentation of crime. In both Howard Hawks' *The Big Sleep* (1946) and Otto Preminger's *Where the Sidewalk Ends* (1950) the gangsters are shadowy, marginal figures, but the most menacing in the former is called Canino and the gangleader in the latter Scalisi, both Italian names. In Richard Wilson's *Al Capone* (1959) the coffin of racketeer Big Jim Colosimo is borne by, on the one side gangsters, and on the other politicians. Henry Hathaway's *Kiss of Death* (1947), Robert Siodmak's *Cry of the City* (1949), Gordon Douglas' *Kiss Tomorrow Goodbye* (1951) and Fritz Lang's *The Big Heat* (1953) include corrupt lawyers and/or policemen. The reasons for these and other conventions lie deep in American social history.

American commitment to individualism and success is represented in economic terms by *laissez-faire* capitalism and in political terms by attachment to States' rights. In the period of rapid industrialisation following the end of the Civil War, these two factors were significant in determining the quality of the vast cities which grew up at this time. The furious growth associated with unfettered capitalism attracted most of the immigrants to large cities such as New York and Chicago, where freedom from control by the central government led to the emergence of the boss system in city politics and to a

Politics and crime: racketeer's coffin borne by gangsters and politicians in *Al Capone*

tradition of civic corruption faithfully reflected in the gangster film.

Several commentators have pointed out that the puritan element in American life has consistently caused legislation to be enacted against human desires and failings; hence the early and widespread legislation against gambling and prostitution – two of the first areas, together with strong-arm politics, to be taken over by racketeers and gangsters. What was perhaps the final convulsion of American puritanism resulted in the Volstead Act (1919), whereby the manufacture and sale of alcoholic beverages, except for medicinal purposes, became illegal. This, more than any other event, gave American crime its impulse to cartelisation. Prohibition lasted until 1933, and the earliest gangster films (1930–32), and many of the Fifties and Sixties reconstructions, deal with this period in which gang wars were fought largely to decide who controlled a city's drinking.

The pattern of immigration in the nineteenth century gave rise to what Daniel Bell has called ethnic succession; that is, as each ethnic group entered America in large numbers it automatically occupied the bottom rung on the social ladder. By the time the Italian immigrants came in the 1880s, much of the political control of the large northern urban centres was in the hands of the Irish, who had come increasingly since the great famine of the 1840s. Deprived of the political patronage necessary to rise to the top, many Italian immigrants ascended on what Bell has called 'the queer ladder of social mobility': crime. The most notorious name of the Prohibition period was that of Al Capone; and of the three major gangster films of the first phase, two (*Little Caesar* and *Scarface*) are about Italian gangsters, establishing a convention still apparent in the genre.

From the Prohibition period onwards, the gangster film has leaned heavily on the reality of American crime. Vast criminal organisations had been built to circumvent Prohibition, and when the Volstead Act was repealed in 1933 they looked round for a new source of income. They found this primarily in industrial racketeering, which was practised in several ways: by hiring out protection both to employers and unions, by gaining control of unions and shaking down industry to prevent strikes, and by extortion from vulnerable industries (e.g. fruit, cleaning and dyeing) to avoid 'accidents' to their stock. When the central figure in Don Siegel's Thirties reconstruction, *Baby Face Nelson* (1957), is released from jail he is taken to the local crime boss, Rocca, who tells him that repeal has killed the booze business, but offers him a contract to kill a union organiser. The theme of labour racketeering found its way into Thirties gangster films as well, notably in Lloyd Bacon's *Racket Busters* (1938), and was still around in the Fifties in Elia Kazan's *On the Waterfront* and Vincent Sherman's *The Garment Jungle*.

Particular plot elements in the Thirties were dependent on real events. There was a short cycle of films about kidnapping, no doubt stimulated by the Lindbergh case, and the theme

reappears in Roger Corman's Thirties reconstruction *Machine-Gun Kelly*. The publicity-minded J. Edgar Hoover, Director of the Federal Bureau of Investigation, offered his keen collaboration on the G-man cycle of films. The figure of the Special Prosecutor becomes common in the cinema after New York's appointment of Thomas E. Dewey to such a post in 1935. At a deeper level, the preoccupation of many gangster films of the late Thirties with the social origins of crime and the possibility of the criminal's reform is surely traceable to the increased interest in sociology during the Depression, and in particular to the work of the Chicago school of sociology in which the pioneering figures were Robert Park and Jane Addams. More centrally, however, under the Roosevelt coalition the city rather than the country became the strategic place for capturing the big vote. The movement of the city to the centre of the political stage hastened its recognition in social terms, so that

'The final convulsion of American puritanism': (*left*) Robert Stack in *The Scarface Mob*; (*above*) David Janssen in *The Big Bankroll*

(*above*) National aspirations and religious traditions. Little Italy in *Pay or Die*; (*below*) Labour racketeering in *Racket Busters*

Politics, corruption and violence in the city: *The Racket*

works as apparently disparate as the historian Arthur M. Schlesinger's *The Rise of the City* (1933) and Michael Curtiz's film *Angels With Dirty Faces* (1938) were both, in fact, responses to the growing importance of the city and its attendant problems.

Had the gangster film rather than the thriller dominated the Forties, it would doubtless have concentrated on gambling, since large-scale general labour racketeering was smashed in 1943 and the criminal organisations then vied for control of the racing wire and other gambling operations. Abraham Polonsky's *Force of Evil* (1949) deals with one aspect of gambling, the numbers racket, and it faithfully reflects the quasi-respectability of the Forties racketeer. The gangster, Ben Tucker, having made his money by violent means during the Prohibition period, does not muscle in on the numbers racket, but employs a Wall Street attorney to organise his takeover bid. The leading gangster figure in Jacques Tourneur's *Out of the Past* (1947) is presented as a gambler, and the prominence of gambling in racketeering in the Forties may help to explain the ubiquitousness of the night-club owner, operating crooked wheels and marked decks, as a villain in the thrillers of the period.

Some critics have attempted to relate the gangster film and thriller to American culture in more general ways. Both can be seen as the culmination of a long tradition of fervent anti-urbanism in American thought and art, explicit in the work of Jefferson, Emerson, Thoreau, Hawthorne, Melville, Poe, Henry Adams, Henry James and William Dean Howells, and implicit in the city novels of Theodore Dreiser and Upton Sinclair. This is, of course, the reverse of the coin of the American commitment to agrarianism which seeps into other aspects of American cinema, most notably the Western. The perceptive Robert Warshow saw the gangster film (and, incidentally, jazz and the anarchic comedy of the Marx Brothers) as an unusual rejection, within popular art, of the optimism of American culture:

... the gangster is the 'no' to that great American 'yes' which is stamped so big over our official culture and yet has so little to do with the way we really feel about our lives.

As the gangster lies dead in the street at the end of almost every gangster movie, his death reassures us, Warshow suggests, in our inevitable failure. If Warshow's conclusion is somewhat speculative, he rightly draws attention to the gangster's compulsive drive for success and its relationship to the value pattern of 'normal' American society. He also indicates the way in which the thriller must be discussed in any attempt to relate it to American culture. It is useless to try to align the wholly fictitious events of the thriller with actual events. However, it is possible to speculate on the reasons for the emergence of the thriller as *film noir* in 1941 and for its continued survival in the post-war period. On one level, the great crash on Wall Street in 1929, the Depression and the rise of Fascism in Europe can be seen to have influenced the American cinema in general in its production, especially during the late 1930s, of socially conscious films such as *Winterset, Mr Deeds Goes to Town, The Grapes of Wrath* and the socially oriented gangster films discussed in Chapter 3. However, this obvious interest in the workings of society was accompanied, indeed stimulated, by a general mood of fear and insecurity, by the feeling that the formerly rigid laws of politics and economics were dissolving and that the future involved only uncertainty. It seems reasonable to suggest that this uncertainty is paralleled in the general mood of malaise, the loneliness and *angst* and the lack of clarity about the characters' motives in the thriller. It seems reasonable, too, to suggest that its continuance into the post-war period was stimulated by the uncertainty of the Cold War, that its misogyny was connected with the heightened desirability and concomitant suspicion of women back home experienced by men at war, and that its obvious cruelty was related to the mood of a society to whom the horrors of Auschwitz and Hiroshima and other atrocities of the Second World War had just been revealed. Where *Angels With Dirty Faces* (1938) represents a statement of general concern about the social origins of crime, *The Dark Corner* (1946) is a cry of loneliness and despair in a sick world. The hero of the latter states at one point, 'I'm backed up in a dark corner and I don't know who's hitting me.' This shift from the social to the personal has been noted in the re-emergence of the gangster film in the post-war period, where, characteristically, the hero is faced with a moral dilemma about his own relationship to the criminal milieu.

Also, if the Thirties, for American cinema, was the era of popularised Marx, the Forties was the time of diluted Freud. Dreams, nightmares, hysteria, madness are recurrent themes in the *films noirs* of the Forties, often expressed in explicitly Freudian terms. For example, in *Fear in the Night*, in an apparent nightmare, the central figure murders his authoritarian surrogate father, his detective brother-in-law. The figure of the psychiatrist becomes central: in *The Dark Mirror* (1946), for instance. And he even takes his place, in the shape of Warner Baxter's Crime Doctor, alongside other private investigators of the time.

There are also good reasons within the film industry why the black thriller should so dominate the Forties. Several film-makers, most notably Fritz Lang, Robert Siodmak and Billy Wilder, had fled from Europe in the Thirties, and their sensibilities, forged in the uncertainty of Weimar Germany and decaying Austria-Hungary, were much more sour and pessimistic than the more buoyant vision of native American directors such as Ford and Capra. These immigrant directors found within the thriller, and the *film noir* generally, a congenial means of expression.

The Fifties gangster film maintained its connection with the reality of American crime, in that the dominant motif of the decade, the syndicate, was adopted from two events: the smashing of a national murder organisation by a New York district attorney, Burton Turkus (the theme of *Murder Inc.*), and the revelations in 1951 of the Senate Special Committee to Investigate Organised Crime in Inter-State Commerce, often called the Kefauver Committee after its chairman. The latter suggested that there was a national criminal organisation and that it was called the Mafia, a secret society originating as an anti-Bourbon group in late eighteenth-century Sicily and imported to the USA by the waves of Italian immigrants from the 1880s onwards. The American cinema reflected a national predisposition to look for conspiracies, and the Mafia became part of the gangster film. It was often referred to as the Syndicate or the Organisation, but sometimes it was named, as in Edward L. Cahn's *Inside the Mafia* (1959), which identified that organisation with the big-time criminals arrested at what appears to have been a crime convention in Apalachin, New York, in 1957.

However, the name Mafia has been thrown around very

The influence of the Kefauver Committee: *Hoodlum Empire* (Forrest Tucker)

loosely in the cinema and often used to describe quite separate Italian-American criminal organisations such as the Black Hand, Camorra and L'Unione Siciliano. Only Roger Corman's *The St Valentine's Day Massacre* attempts to outline the solely Sicilian constitution of the Mafia and its relationship with non-Sicilian criminals such as Capone. Other gangster films mentioning the Mafia have tended to concentrate on its more ritualistic conventions such as *omerta* (simplified for the screen to a code of silence) and the implanting of a kiss by the executioner on the cheek of his victim. No film has taken heed of the serious criticism of the Kefauver findings, such as that voiced by Daniel Bell and by the California Crime Commission of 1953. Bell disagrees that the Mafia is at the centre of organised crime in America and considers the predominance of Italian names in crime as due to a peculiar interrelationship of sociological factors, Italian immigration, the

Crime as big business: Broderick Crawford chairs a Syndicate meeting in *New York Confidential*

nature of the American economy and the politics of American cities. The California Crime Commission concluded that there is a national crime consortium, but that, while based on the Unione Siciliano, it regards commercial gain as more important than racial purity and is now inter-ethnic.

After the syndicate phase, the gangster film reached back into its own history with the series of historical reconstructions which appeared in the late Fifties and early Sixties. The refurbished Forties thrillers now being made would seem to merit the same comments, regarding their relationship to American culture, as their originals of the Forties; but later film critics and historians, at a greater distance, may perceive in them something quintessentially of their decade.

# 5: Fritz Lang

Fritz Lang's art is the most uncompromisingly bleak in all cinema. Born in Vienna in 1890, he studied painting and architecture before serving on the Western front in the First World War. This experience, his own tribal *angst*, and the general malaise which affected European, particularly German, artists and intellectuals in the Twenties, led him, as he has written, to make 'a fetish of tragedy'. The mood of terror apparent in German silent cinema of the Twenties is well exemplified in Lang's work, and both *Dr Mabuse* (1922) and *Metropolis* (1926) display the despair of mankind, the sense of evil and of omnipotent forces at work, which forms the necessary starting-point for an understanding of Lang's films. In these films the evil forces are manifest in the abstractions of the power-mad tyrant, Mabuse, and in the slave city of Metropolis, but they might just as easily come from within man, as in Lang's first sound film *M* (1932), a study of the Düsseldorf child-murderer, tortured by his own evil impulses: 'I want to run away. I have to run away. I am always forced to move along streets, and someone is always behind me. It is I, I am myself behind me, and yet I cannot escape.' Since Lang sees man as persecuted both without and within, by forces he cannot control, it is scarcely surprising that he should examine repeatedly man's most characteristic acts, sexuality and violence, or that he should demonstrate again and again the pitiful unsoundness of man's most cherished institution, the law.

Refusing Goebbels' offer of control of the Third Reich's film industry, Lang fled Germany in 1933, going first to France and then, in 1934, to America, where he had an extremely productive working life of twenty years from 1936 to 1956. It is difficult to resist the conviction that the physical presence of urban America and the country's *mores* confirmed Lang's despair. The pessimistic cast of his vision, and the nature of Hollywood film production, led him to contribute substantially to the area of cinema discussed in this book, though he himself made few films which could be called unequivocally gangster films or thrillers.

Lang is fascinated with the whole process of the criminal life, but especially with detection and conviction. His policemen are formidable figures – Lohmann in *M*, Bannion in *The Big Heat* (1953) – contemptuous of the due processes of law, and at times even menacing in appearance, like Inspector Prentice in *Ministry of Fear* (1944), who is bleakly present paring his fingernails like James Joyce's God, or the furies of *You Only Live Once* (1936), who appear with the utmost suddenness in black and bearing machine-guns and rifles. Lang depicts minutely the search for clues leading to the identity of the murderer in *M*, the deliberate laying of clues pointing to Tom Garret as the murderer in *Beyond a Reasonable Doubt* (1956), the blackmailer's expert search for the hidden fountain-pen in *Woman in the Window* (1944), and Bannion's investigations into the identity of his wife's killers in *The Big Heat*. But it is in his depiction of the judicial process that Lang's pessimism is most apparent. Court scenes recur in many of his films, and in every case the rigour, pomp and platitudes of the law are exposed as shallow and unrelated to the real forces which shape men's lives. In *M* the judges, jury and officers of the court are criminals and underworld figures; in *Fury* (1936) the law is used for the purpose of personal vengeance; in *You Only Live Once* the court sentences an innocent man to death –

this recurs in *Scarlet Street* (1945). And in *Beyond a Reasonable Doubt* the law is duped in two ways – it is shown to be capable of convicting an innocent man, and at the same time it is used as an instrument by a guilty man in an attempt to escape punishment.

It is useful to outline the plot strategy of *Beyond a Reasonable Doubt* since it is central to an understanding of Lang's work. Tom Garret (Dana Andrews) is the prospective son-in-law of a newspaper proprietor violently opposed to capital punishment. The newspaper proprietor believes that he will prove the case for the abolition of the death penalty if he can demonstrate conclusively that the law could convict an innocent man of murder. The strangled body of a burlesque dancer is found, and the newspaper proprietor prevails on Garret to pretend to be guilty, laying innumerable clues in his car, at the scene of the crime, and by other means such as having no alibi. The newspaper proprietor documents the laying of the clues in writing and photographs. Garret is arrested, tried and sentenced to death. The newspaper proprietor sets out for the District Attorney's office with the evidence of Garret's innocence, but he is killed in a car crash and the evidence is destroyed. His daughter fights to prove Garret's innocence and manages to find out something about the burlesque dancer's past, but when Garret is told this he mentions the dead girl by her former name, indicating that he had known her, and, by extension, that he is in fact guilty of the murder. By this time fresh evidence from the newspaper proprietor's safe establishes his apparent innocence, but his fiancée informs the prison governor of his guilt and his reprieve is withheld.

Put baldly, the plot seems incredibly artificial, the outcome depending on three chance events, the death of the newspaper proprietor, Garret's slip of the tongue, and the finding of the new evidence; but in fact such elements of apparent chance are an integral part of Lang's vision, another cruel force by which man is tortured, forever offered salvation when he has taken an irreversible step the other way. Such multiple ironies of fate recur in Lang's work. Eddie Taylor (Henry Fonda), the innocent man condemned to die in *You Only Live Once*, gets out of the condemned cell and, as proof of his innocence is established and a pardon rushed through, kills the prison chaplain and escapes. He is hunted without mercy for this killing and shot dead when he has taken his first steps in apparent freedom, over the border in Canada. Richard Wanley (Edward G. Robinson), the respectable professor of *The Woman in the Window*, is implicated in a murder. Believing his future to be ruined, he takes poison and, dying, fails to answer the telephone which brings the news that the blackmailer is dead and his own future intact. By an added irony, the action of the film turns out to be a dream dreamt by the professor. Critics have attacked this device, but it should be recalled that before his dream Professor Wanley is seen lecturing on Freud; and the events of his dream may not be far removed from his real desires.

Inevitably, violence looms large in Lang's work. Often – though by no means exclusively – it achieves a sexual dimension by being directed against women. Lang makes frequent use of strangulation, an act which places murderer and victim in close bodily proximity, like an embrace. The victims in *M* are little girls. In *Scarlet Street, Beyond a Reasonable Doubt* and, up to a point, in *The Big Heat*, they are the *femmes fatales* so characteristic of American cinema in the immediate postwar period and going back ultimately to German silent cinema. The violence they suffer is often presented as man's revenge upon their cold, provocative sexuality.

With destructive impulses coming as much from within man as from without, the borders of respectability and criminality are ill-defined. When the lynch mob on trial in *Fury* see on the newsreel what they became, they are aghast; the garage attendants in *You Only Live Once* rob the cash register, knowing that the fugitive Taylors will be blamed for it; and the solid bourgeois figures of *Scarlet Street* and *Woman in the Window* are destroyed by their own capacity for sexual enslavement. Distinctions between guilt and innocence, good and

The strangulation motif: Glenn Ford in *The Big Heat*

evil, criminality and legality, are blurred. Often the functions of the police and the criminals are deliberately confused, as in *M*. In subtler visual terms, the audience's certainty that it can distinguish the criminals from the police may be undermined, as in *The Big Heat*.

Formally and thematically, Lang's art is highly artificial. He never explores his characters' psychology in depth, preferring to manipulate them schematically to illustrate his own metaphysical position, the *angst* and fatalism of which is emphasised by his non-naturalistic style, prevailing darkness cut by slabs of light, brooding shadows, a fondness for a baroque reduplication of images by means of mirrors, concentration within scenes on apparently unimportant details which evoke a profound sense of unease (the frogs in *You Only Live Once*, the train wheels in *Fury*) and, on occasion, the use of totally symbolic elements (the juxtaposition of cackling hens with gossiping women in *Fury*).

It is a pity that Lang did not submit himself more frequently to the discipline of genre, for this discipline resulted in his most formally restrained and beautifully constructed film, *The Big Heat*, in which the narrative proceeds apace but each scene is resonant with subtle, characteristically Langian meanings. The swift opening sequences indicate the major motifs of the film and demonstrate that Lang is one of the cleanest craftsmen in the cinema.

The opening image is a close-up of a ·38 revolver, a fitting image for this most violent of films and also one that places it squarely within the tradition of the gangster film. Then, in following the narrative, what the audience sees is a series of telephone calls: Bertha Duncan calls Mike Lagana, who in turn speaks on the telephone to Debbie and Vince Stone. The telephoning is thus a narrative device which, with the utmost economy, allows Lang to introduce his audience to the major figures (with the exception of the central character, Bannion). The themes of the film, on the other hand, are carried in what the characters say (the theme of official corruption) and in what

'A fitting image for this most violent of films . . .': the opening shot of *The Big Heat*

Lang tells his audience about them, and the quality of their relationships, by his use of casting, playing, dress, décor and lighting. Lagana is first seen in silk pyjamas in a softly lit, suffocatingly luxurious bed attended by a handsome young man in a white dressing-gown who serves him like an acolyte, handing him the telephone, lighting his cigarette. The scene expresses Lagana's wealth and position, the quality of domination in his relationships, and hints at his aberrant sexuality. Debbie is first seen, clad in silk pyjamas, stretched out on a couch. The casting of Gloria Grahame in the role, her dress and deportment, all act to give the audience the information that will allow them to place her in the tradition of the gangster's moll. Similarly, Vince Stone's opulent apartment, his garish dress, the fact that he is played by Lee Marvin, and his poker playing, all place him as a gangster. Also, within this scene, the dominating quality of his relationship with Debbie is stressed.

The image opening the scene in which Bannion is introduced also fits into the iconography of communications devices so common to the gangster genre. A police photographer taking shots of Tom Duncan's corpse gives way to Sergeant Dave Bannion conducting the investigation into the suicide. Again the casting of Glenn Ford brings much force to the character: his grim, unsmiling playing, and his brutal shape in battered hat and long trench-coat, are instantly expressive and typical of the genre. Bannion is the central figure in the film, and it is his movement from policeman to avenger after the murder of his wife which carries the weight of thematic interest. In fact it is a restatement of the theme of *Fury* and what was to become the theme of *Beyond a Reasonable Doubt*, the blurring of distinctions between criminality and legality, good and evil, right and wrong.

Bannion's relationship with his wife must be seen in contrast to the other pair relationships shown or implied in the film. The central element, stressed in their actions and in the dialogue, is of their sharing things — cigarettes, beer and food. Unlike the relationships of the other pairs, Lagana/George, Vince/Debbie, and by implication Bertha Duncan/Tom Duncan, this is a relationship based on equality, not dominance. There is also a contrast, expressed in décor and lighting, between the Bannion home and those of the others. In contrast to the darkness of the Duncan home, Bannion's is brightly lit; in contrast to the luxury of Lagana's and Stone's places, Bannion's home is plain. The Bannion home is extremely important as a measure of his hardening soul, for into it the violence of his job progressively intrudes, first in a telephone call about Duncan's girl in the middle of his dinner, then the anonymous obscene call telling him to lay off investigating the Duncan suicide, and finally in the killing of his wife. Significantly, his leaving home, where his humanity has been defined, is one of the turning-points in his move towards violence and criminality. He goes to live in the twilight world of anonymous apartments inhabited by gangsters such as Larry Gordon, a world described

'Sisters under the mink': gangster's moll (Gloria Grahame) and cop's widow (Jeanette Nolan) in *The Big Heat*

architecturally by Debbie as 'early nothing'. When Bannion resigns from the police he turns in his badge but, significantly, retains his gun. He has become the avenger, indistinguishable in behaviour from the criminals he hunts.

The theme of the blurring of the distinctions between law and crime, respectability and non-respectability, is carried by other figures and situations in the film, often in dialogue and image simultaneously; as when Debbie and Bertha Duncan confront each other and Debbie describes them as 'sisters under the mink', or in the figure of Lieutenant Wilks, who will take no initiative against crime because of his imminent retirement, or even in the patrolman, detailed with several others to guard Lagana's house, who says he just does what he's told. The theme achieves its most subtle and unnerving statement in the scene in which Bannion, having learned that the police guard has been taken off his brother-in-law's house where his

'The underlying echo of de Sade . . .': Gloria Grahame in *The Big Heat*

child is staying, goes there, and climbing the stairs is confronted by a figure emerging from the shadows. The actor playing the role, his dress, the lighting of the scene, all combine to suggest that he is one of Lagana's men. In fact he is an ex-army friend of Bannion's brother-in-law taking over from the police.

The violence in *The Big Heat* is particularly horrifying, and is directed primarily against women. Its horror is cumulative: Lucy Chapman is tortured and strangled off-screen, Mrs Bannion is killed off-screen, though the audience hears an explosion and sees Bannion drag her from the wrecked car, and the bar-fly's hand is burned by Vince Stone on-screen. The most horrifying act of all is Vince Stone's scalding of Debbie's face with boiling coffee. The underlying echo of de Sade becomes explicit when Debbie, dying on the floor, covers her disfigured face with her fur coat.

'. . . a figure emerging from the shadows': Bannion (Glenn Ford) confronted in *The Big Heat*

There have traditionally been pressures on the Hollywood film-maker to end his films on an optimistic note, and those of darker sensibility, such as Lang, have often made the endings of their films apparently optimistic, but incorporating an equivocal element. Such is the case with *The Big Heat*. The criminals are arrested or killed, the syndicate is smashed, and Bannion is reinstated in the police department. However, amid the scenes of congratulation a message comes through about a hit-and-run accident. Bannion and his associate go out on the case. The bleak cycle has begun once more.

# 6: John Huston

'If you want fresh air don't look for it in this town.'
Louis Ciavelli in *The Asphalt Jungle*

The meaning of some artists, such as Luis Buñuel or Samuel Fuller, is located primarily in their themes; of others, like Robert Siodmak or Georges Franju, in their style. John Huston is a puzzling case. He has defined his approach to film-making as follows:

... I don't seek to interpret, to put my own stamp on the material. I try to be as faithful to the original material as I can ... In fact, it's the fascination that I feel for the original that makes me want to make it into a film ... The most important element to me is always the idea that I'm trying to express, and everything technical is only a method to make the idea into clear form.

Huston's apparent commitment to content rather than form (to use inadequate but generally understood polarities) raises problems for the critic who attempts to define Huston's vision in terms of his style. The austere, pared down, functional style of *The Maltese Falcon*, *The Treasure of Sierra Madre* and *The Asphalt Jungle*, so highly praised by James Agee, changes in relation to the source material. *The Red Badge of Courage* was shot with Matthew Brady's Civil War photographs in mind, and *Moby Dick* was photographed in black and white overprinted with colour to suggest old whaling prints. *Freud* experiments with soft focus and Bergmanesque bleaching, and *Reflections in a Golden Eye* and part of *The Bible* were conceived as being suffused with a golden light. Thus the critic would be hard pressed to define the stylistic continuity between Huston's early and late work. This has meant that attempts to reveal Huston's vision have concentrated largely on his themes which, in their turn, have arguably proved as variable as his style. Several French critics, stout defenders of the early Huston, have become angry or dejected by the development of the Huston hero from aggressive extrovert to tortured introvert, and have seen Huston's career as a decline. This is substantially the view of Gilles Jacob in the chapter on Huston in his *Cinéma Moderne* (Lyon: Serdoc, 1964). Only Paul Mayersberg in his brave but ultimately unconvincing review article on *Reflections in a Golden Eye* in *Movie 15* suggests that there is a thematic continuity throughout Huston's work.

Mayersberg mentions specifically that the animal world has played a large part in Huston's films (the end of *The Asphalt Jungle*, the imagery of *Night of the Iguana*, *Moby Dick*, *The Misfits*, *The List of Adrian Messenger*, *The Roots of Heaven*); that impossible love relationships recur (*The African Queen*, *Moulin Rouge*, *Heaven Knows Mr Allison*, *The Barbarian and the Geisha* and *The Misfits*); and that the hard, physical adventurers of the early films, and the adventurers in the psyche of later films, are the head and tail of the same coin: the two sides of Huston. While it is undoubtedly true that Huston as a man loves the animal world (his service in the Mexican cavalry and his riding to hounds in Galway) it is difficult to see this as anything more than incidental to his work (as in *The List of Adrian Messenger*), or at the most as a source of imagery for defining some men's ideals (Dix in *The Asphalt Jungle*). Set against Mayersberg's claim is Huston's insistence on his fidelity to his literary sources; the fact that these sources have, as his career developed, become increasingly 'serious' (Stephen Crane and Herman Melville as opposed to Dashiell Hammet; Arthur Miller, Tennessee Williams and Carson McCullers rather than W. R. Burnett); and that *Night of the Iguana*, for example, is still primarily *about* spiritual masochism, hardly a recurrent theme in Huston's work.

Clearly, then, the critic making a case for Huston as *auteur* has no easy task. *Auteur*-oriented critics are fond of quoting Renoir's remark that the film-maker makes the same archetypal movie over and over again. While they are prepared to admit the possibility of the artist developing within a set of themes – as, say, John Ford demonstrably does – they are loath to accept the notion quite common among art critics that an artist's work might fall into discernible periods, each of which contains related works but which, taken separately, bear little relationship to each other. It is with a critical schema such as this that Huston's development makes most sense.

The relevant period for this study is from 1941 to 1950, the relevant films *The Maltese Falcon, In This Our Life, Across the Pacific, The Treasure of Sierra Madre, Key Largo, We Were Strangers* and *The Asphalt Jungle*. Appropriately, the period opens and closes with classic genre pieces. *Key Largo* is, in a sense, a gangster film, but its gangsters vegetate in an alien milieu, a Florida hotel, and the dramatic impulse is clearly to present Maxwell Anderson's very verbose play about the necessity of moral choice (a dominant theme of the period) rather than to create the dense surface texture of grim cityscapes and violent action of the gangster film. The mood of this period of Huston's work is summed up in the final images of *The Treasure of Sierra Madre*, in which the gold dust the prospectors have torn from the mountain, which has set them apart from each other and caused the deaths of several men, blows back across the desert towards its source while the old prospector (Walter Huston, the director's father) laughs crazily as it goes. In the films of this period effort is futile, betrayal is likely, failure is certain.

There is a scene in *The Maltese Falcon* in which Sam Spade (Humphrey Bogart) is being interviewed by the District Attorney in connection with two murders. The D.A. assures him that if he has nothing to conceal he has nothing to fear, and

Spade replies, 'Everyone has something to conceal.' This remark could stand as a text for *The Maltese Falcon*, in which nothing is as it seems: personal identities are shifting and uncertain, relationships are characterised by duplicity and even objects prove false. Thus Brigid O'Shaughnessy (Mary Astor) is also known as Wonderly and Le Blanc, and Joel Cairo (Peter Lorre) carries Swiss, French and British passports; Brigid betrays Thursby, Archer and Spade, and is in turn betrayed by Spade; and Caspar Guttman (Sydney Greenstreet) allows his protégé Wilmer Cook (Elisha Cook Jnr) to be used as a fall guy ('If you lose a son it is possible to gain another. There is only one Maltese Falcon'). The overall theme of the film is encapsulated in the scenes in which Guttman and Spade discuss the terms under which the latter will hand over the precious carving. Spade has lied systematically to Guttman, pretending to have the bird, doubling the price he has been offered by Cairo, and even simulating anger to force the negotiations to a conclusion. Guttman, for his part, repeatedly expresses admiration for Spade's forthrightness ('You're the man for me, sir, no beating about the bush') while waiting for the drug he has put in Spade's drink to take effect. One of the recurrent motifs of the film is Spade's attempt to establish facts: he urges Joel Cairo to put his cards on the table, he systematically makes characters repeat accounts of events in order to perceive their logic, and his immediate reaction to a dead (Jacobi) or unconscious (Cairo) body is to search it for identifying documents.

The casting of Bogart as Spade is one of the great triumphs of the film, so fully does he, physically, recapitulate the qualities of Spade's world. Naturally he brings precisely the same physical qualities to the role of Philip Marlowe in *The Big Sleep*, which evokes a similar world to that of *The Maltese Falcon*; and the rightness of his physical style for this role can be measured against George Montgomery's Philip Marlowe in *The High Window*. Further comparisons could be made with Dick Powell's and Robert Montgomery's versions in *Farewell, My Lovely* and *Lady in the Lake* respectively. As has been

Fact-finding: Bogart as Sam Spade checks one of Joel Cairo's passports in *The Maltese Falcon*

noted already, there is a tradition in the American cinema of exteriorising qualities of character by casting, a process which the American cinema arrived at intuitively and which Eisenstein theorised on and practised so brilliantly in the Russian cinema.

While the sickness of *The Maltese Falcon's* world is carried largely through the physical grotesquerie of its characters, it is conveyed also in the hints of their aberrant sexuality: Guttman, in silk dressing-gown, takes Spade's arm and places his hand on his knee; Cairo, with his gardenia-scented calling card and flirtatious manner, had a shady past, Brigid recalls, with a boy in Istanbul. Even the sexual encounters between Spade and Brigid are fraught with unease and potential violence. Spade kisses her at one point with his hands round her throat. At his apartment, as he bends to kiss her, the camera lifts to the open window to disclose the menacing figure of Wilmer Cook waiting in the street. Sam Spade pays a heavy price, in human terms, for inhabiting this world. He has ambivalent relationships with the police (Lieutenant Dundy suspects him of killing Miles Archer); and he is having an affair with his partner's wife. He is interested primarily in money, and there are several transactions with Spade on the receiving end, often upping the figure offered by the other party, as when his stony lack of response to Miss Wonderly's hundred dollars causes her hurriedly to add another hundred, and when, offered a retainer by Cairo ('You will take, say, one hundred dollars?') he replies, 'No, I will take, say, two hundred dollars.' As he later tells Brigid about their first meeting, 'We didn't believe your story, we believed your money.' Yet it would be wrong to describe Spade as wholly amoral. There is a vestige of principle as well as professionalism behind his remark, 'If a man's partner is killed he's supposed to do something about it.' But the professionalism is reinforced by his outlining his reasons for turning Brigid over to the police (principally that she might decide to kill him some time later because he knows too much). His most conspicuous quality, his capacity for survival, emerges in his remark to Brigid, 'I'll have some rotten nights after I've sent you over, but that will pass.' As the lift gate closes, prison-like, on Brigid, Spade walks out holding the Maltese Falcon. 'What's that?' asks Detective-Sergeant Polhaus. 'The stuff that dreams are made of,' replies Spade, hugging the fool's gold.

The world of *The Asphalt Jungle* is less suffocating and mysterious, but no less bleak than that of *The Maltese Falcon*. Gilles Jacob, commending Huston for having contributed to the humanising of the gangster film, describes it as a world in which men have families and earn their daily bread. Certainly the impulse behind the characters' involvement in the jewel robbery is not the compulsive criminality, the desire for success, of the Thirties gangster. For many of them it is the means to realise a dream: for Doc Riedenschneider (Sam Jaffe) it means Mexico and a paradise of pretty girls, for Louis Ciavelli (Anthony Caruso) an end to the problem of 'mouths to feed,

Obsessions in *The Asphalt Jungle*: Louis Calhern and Marilyn Monroe, and (*below*) Sam Jaffe

rent to pay', for Alonzo Emmerich (Louis Calhern) 'a plane to another country, another life', and for Dix (Sterling Hayden) it means Hickory Wood Farm in Kentucky, where he lived as a boy.

Huston's view of his characters in *The Asphalt Jungle*, unlike his detached attitude in *The Maltese Falcon*, is strikingly sympathetic. Dix, throwing the money he owes at Cobby's feet, is demonstrated to be a man of honour who can inspire the friendship of Gus and Doc and the dog-like devotion of Doll. Doc, despite his fondness for young girls and pin-ups, is a man of dignity and humour, and even Emmerich, the initiator of the cycle of betrayals which engulfs the characters, has an extremely tender relationship with his 'niece' Angela. Huston deliberately draws attention to his characters' humanity by juxtaposing them, through montage, with harsh comments made on them by figures outside their world. From Mrs Emmerich's remark to her husband, 'When I think of all these people you associate with, downright criminals, I get scared,' Huston dissolves to Dix and Doc, whom the audience have learned to understand and admire; and from the Police Commissioner's harsh judgment on Dix, 'a hardened killer, a hooligan, a man without human feeling or mercy,' there is a dissolve to Dix, without 'enough blood in him to keep a chicken alive' on his last obsessional journey to Kentucky. In contrast to Huston's obvious sympathy for the gangsters, particularly Dix and Doc, the police are presented with varying degrees of hostility. The Police Commissioner, a draconian enforcer of the law, offers in his press conference the polarities of clemency and justice; the corrupt and brutal Dietrich betrays both the police and the criminals from whom he has been 'on the take'; and the rank and file policemen are seen most dramatically when, hunting Louis Ciavelli, they kick open the door of his house and disclose his wife and family round his open coffin.

The overall progression of Huston's work from a concern with man's actions to an inner concern is restated in the

89

Irony in Huston: the last shot of *The Asphalt Jungle*

development from *The Maltese Falcon* to *The Asphalt Jungle*. The endings of both – like those of most of the films of his first period – are profoundly ironic. But where in *The Maltese Falcon*, while the object of the obsession is proved to be worthless, the possibility of finding a genuine Aladdin's lamp remains open, in *The Asphalt Jungle* Doc Riedenschneider is destroyed by the phantoms in his own psyche, captured by the police as he dallies too long in a diner, fascinated by the body of a dancing girl; and Dix, too, is destroyed as he takes his first steps in Hickory Wood Farm. The tone of the final image of the film sums up a decade of Huston's work: as Dix's lifeless body lies in the grass, the horses he talked about endlessly, and lost all his money playing, trot towards him and encircle his body.

# 7: Jules Dassin

Despite the largely formalist orientation of most art and much criticism today, the artist continues to view himself in Romantic terms; that is, believing his prime responsibility to be to his own act of creation rather than to the necessity of communicating with his audience or to the rules of pre-existing artistic forms. He would regard himself as producing his best art when least trammelled. In terms of the cinema, the notion of freely choosing to work within popular genres such as the Western or the gangster film would be anathema to him. Jules Dassin's career could be partly seen as illustrating the dilemma of the Romantic view.

Dassin has often expressed the view that his films up to 1955 were routine assignments in which he was not fully involved. He worked within the Hollywood system from 1941 to 1949, came to London in 1950 to make *Night and the City* for an American company, spent five lean years in Paris unable to work because his name was on the Hollywood blacklist, and made *Rififi*, a gangster film, in Paris in 1955. Since *Celui Qui Doit Mourir* (1957) he has had virtually complete artistic control of the films he has made. Dassin would doubtless be surprised to hear the critical opinion that his pre-1957 work is, on the whole, better than his later work, that films of both periods frequently display the same stylistic and thematic preoccupations, and that the same drives which lent depth and interest to his earlier work have led to excess and self-indulgence in the later films.

The key film for understanding the reasons for Dassin's decline as an artist is the excellent *Two Smart People* (1946). Ace Connors (John Hodiak) and Ricki Woodner (Lucille Ball) are swindlers, each of whom sinks the other's attempt to cheat a rich man. Ace, hunted by the policeman Simms (Lloyd Nolan) after stealing government bonds, decides to serve a five-year jail sentence and live on the proceeds of the bonds when he gets out. He and Simms start a train journey from California to New York, with Ricki also aboard, hoping to get her hands on the bonds. Up to this point the film is a clean and efficient genre piece in which the relationship between Ace and Simms is given an unusual, almost homosexual depth by the way in which their scenes together are played. But Ace is a dreamer. Having fallen in love with Ricki, he suggests that they stop off for a couple of days in Mexico, Simms along with them. There follows a sequence of startling unreality in which the dream is made fact. Lighting, décor, dress – Ace in white tuxedo, Ricki in a Greek gown – and playing combine to stress the dreamlike quality of the experience.

This is simply a foretaste of a later sequence in which they stop off in New Orleans for Mardi Gras. It is in this sequence, a move into ritual, that Dassin's sensibility achieves freer rein. Ace and Simms take on identities analogous to their real personae, Ace as pirate, Simms as a Bat Masterson figure, and there are several confusions of identity with other revellers. Dassin's Mardi Gras has a hysterical, nightmarish quality. He begins the sequence with a close-up of a grotesque mask, people dance with dummies in their arms (expressing the illusion/reality theme of the sequence), a figure in a wolf's head picks up a screaming girl and runs off with her, and music is supplied by a band of dwarfs. Ace is being stalked by Fly (Elisha Cook Jnr), who also wants the bonds, dressed in a harlequin costume. Several bands of revellers wander the streets tossing harlequin dummies in the air and catching them in blankets.

Ritual humiliation in Dassin's *La Loi*

Fly is shot by Simms and falls from a balcony to be caught in a blanket and carried off, his corpse now and then thrown high in the air.

In *Two Smart People* we see Dassin as a superb craftsman submitting to the disciplines of narrative and genre; yet his impulses to ritual and hysteria find expression in a controlled way, and add a baroque dimension which a less interesting sensibility would not have brought to the film. These impulses to dream, hysteria and ritual reappear, still controlled by narrative and genre, in the later films of his Hollywood period. The convicts in *Brute Force* (1947) have a pin-up on the wall of their cell which each uses to give expression to his sexual fantasies. Nick Garcos (Richard Conte), in the opening scene of *Thieves Highway* (1949), wears a cannibal mask to frighten his fiancée. Harry Fabian (Richard Widmark), in *Night and the City*, hysterically pursues the dream of the easy life ('One break, I'm out of the garbage cans for life').

95

It is clear that Dassin felt that the intense impulses of his sensibility could not find adequate expression within the American cinema. He has since sought to accommodate them within the rituals of more primitive societies: Crete in *Celui Qui Doit Mourir*, southern Italy in *La Loi* (1958), Spain in *10.30 p.m. Summer* (1966); or in a modern restatement of classical myth, *Phaedra* (1962). It is perhaps significant that the first film of his later period, *Celui Qui Doit Mourir*, should involve the arch-ritual of the Christian Passion. A ragged band of refugees from the Turks arrives in a remote Cretan village in which a Passion Play is being performed. The figures cast as Christ, John and Mary Magdalen play out their roles by helping the refugees, and suffer for it, the village priest, the Turkish governor, and the villager cast as Judas in the play being their most ardent tormentors. Thematically, one can see the reaching out towards the 'significant' subject which has marred Dassin's later work; and stylistically, when no longer disciplined by the conventions of the Hollywood genre, he rightly earns Lindsay Anderson's reproof:

His desire to transcend melodrama is obviously sincere; yet his instinct for it constantly betrays him. This is probably his chief problem now as an artist.

It is a problem Dassin has yet to solve.

Apart from *Two Smart People*, Dassin has worked four times in the area covered by this book: *The Naked City* (1948), *Thieves Highway*, *Night and the City* and *Rififi*. More recently he has made *Up Tight* (1968), a film which has certain genre elements but whose racial theme carries it into another and different tradition. There is a strong impulse to social criticism and 'realism' in the location thriller *The Naked City*, but this impulse is found almost wholly in the script (one of the writers was Albert Maltz, a member of the famous Hollywood Ten) rather than in Dassin's *mise en scène*. The police are totally deglamorised and presented either as hard-working old men like Muldoon (Barry Fitzgerald) or as callow enthusiasts like Halloran (Don Taylor). Their success in solving the murder case is presented as a wholly co-operative effort: Muldoon establishes that two men rather than one did the killing, Halloran follows the lead implicating Willie (Ted de Corsia), and another officer produces a stolen jewellery list which links Willie to Frank Niles (Howard Duff).

The social criticism appears as a strong critique of the rich: when Frank Niles, the layabout son of a rich family, reveals that he spent fifty dollars in a night-club, Muldoon exclaims that he supported a wife and three kids for a week on that, and another policeman observes, 'You weren't born on the right side of the tracks.' The rich people in the film are presented either as sexually obsessed (Stoneman), or vain and materialistic, like the society lady who, talking about her jewels, says, 'I love to glitter: it's a fixation.' The parents of the murdered girl come up to the city to identify their daughter's body and, against a harsh background of steel girders and the East River, deliver a diatribe against materialism and the quality of life in the city. It is in the depiction of the city that the script's impulse to realism and Dassin's impulse to hysteria and brutality connect. As in *Up Tight* (1968), the city, for Dassin, means steel rather than concrete, and in the pay-off, Willie, holding his bloody and mauled hand, climbs into the girders of Brooklyn Bridge to be shot from his perch by the police below. It is a critical paradox that this, the least typical of Dassin's films, should receive the most extensive critical approbation. There is more of Dassin in the brief, strangely erotic scene in which Willie works out, surrounded by pin-ups of he-men and cuties, than anywhere else, except the ending. If Dassin is a subversive artist, it is certainly not in the way Senator McCarthy would have understood that term.

*Thieves Highway* reveals a similar split between script and direction. The script is, implicitly at least, an attack on capitalism. The whole trading structure – the action takes place in the

San Francisco wholesale fruit market – is presented as conducive only to vice and violence: A undercuts B and is in turn swindled by C. Yet the visual excitement of the film is in no way connected with this theme: it emerges in the images of the scores of apples rolling down the hillside from the overturned truck, in the cruel eroticism of Rica (Valentina Cortese) playing noughts and crosses with her fingernail on Nick's naked body, in the image of Figlia (Lee J. Cobb), his hand smashed by Nick, strewing money along the bar in a vain attempt to appease his assailant. These last two images connect Dassin's Hollywood work with his work in Europe. In *La Loi*, Brigante (Yves Montand) woos Marietta (Gina Lollobrigida) by stroking her flesh with an open flick-knife; and later Marietta, wearing a crown of banknotes, strews the garret she lives in with money stolen from a German tourist.

*The Naked City* and *Thieves Highway* might be mistaken for social realist documents, but not so *Night and the City*. Coming to London with a rather misleading reputation as a maker of explicit social commentaries, Dassin naturally outraged the British critical fraternity by producing a work the meaning of which is metaphysical. The London of *Night and the City* has no temporal or geographical location; it is Thomson's 'city of dreadful night', Warshow's 'dark, sad city of the imagination'. Its underworld is reminiscent of Villon's Paris or Lang's Düsseldorf: forgers, fences and gangs of organised beggars who draw wooden legs and dark glasses from their patron. The principal recurring image of *Night and the City* is of Harry Fabian, his teeth bared, his eyes staring in terror, as he runs through dark streets in a futile attempt to evade his pursuers. He is a pariah in his own society, the underworld, a man with a price on his head which makes even former friends betray him. 'You're a dead man, Harry Fabian, a dead man,' says the grotesquely obese Noseros (Francis L. Sullivan), striking a cymbal to underline the inevitability of the fact. The physical grotesquerie exemplified in Noseros is central to the meaning

(*above*) 'Cruel eroticism ...': noughts and crosses on the flesh in *Thieves Highway* (Richard Conte, Valentina Cortese); (*below*) physical grotesquerie and non-realistic decor in *Night and the City* (Francis L. Sullivan)

Widmark in *Night and the City*: 'the archetypal modern man . . .

of *Night and the City*, prising it further away from any vestigial connection it might have with a realistic aesthetic. At the beginning of the film Fabian is a club tout, and Kristo (Herbert Lom) a big-time racketeer; they meet in a bizarre world of professional wrestling, inhabited by such grotesque figures as the Strangler (Mike Mazurki) and Gregorius. The ultimate statement of the film is bleak: unlike Figlia in *Thieves Highway*, Kristo remains solidly in control of the city, and Harry Fabian, his life choked out by the Strangler, ends up a carcass in the river. It is significant that Borde and Chaumeton chose as the cover illustration of their *Panorama du Film Noir Américain* a close-up of Harry Fabian. It is easy to see him as the archetypal modern man, running in terror through a dark city.

The delirium and grotesquerie of *Night and the City* can be read as the final spasms of Dassin's sensibility as it writhed

100

... running in terror through a dark city'

within the 'restraints' of the American production system.
From this point onwards, his sensibility is free. But where his
Hollywood films suggest a craftsman who might have become
an artist, most of his European films suggest a talent lost in the
process of trying to create Art.

# 8: Robert Siodmak

Andrew Sarris has noted that Robert Siodmak's American films are more Germanic than his German ones. This apparently simple observation raises complex questions about the collective style of a national cinema in particular periods, the function of genre in determining that style, and the extent to which the artist's stylistic and thematic preoccupations may become subsumed in a genre. Siodmak's case is particularly interesting since he has both a pre- and a post-Hollywood period. If *Menschen am Sonntag* (1929) is taken as representative of his pre-Hollywood period, he would appear then to have been an artist with a neo-realistic aesthetic and a bent for light romance. If *Custer of the West* (1966) is taken as representative of his post-Hollywood phase, it is difficult to locate any artist at all; the film is ponderously naturalistic and stylistically anonymous. On a visual level, neither film bears any relationship to the films Siodmak made in the Hollywood of the Forties. Although American-born, Siodmak was taken back to Germany at an early age by his German parents, made films in Germany and France in the Thirties and came to Hollywood in 1940. By chance there was a fruitful conjunction between the artist and the milieu. Within the *film noir* and the gangster film, Siodmak's style, and therefore his meaning, was moulded.

Siodmak's Hollywood movies are usually called expressionist, and on a superficial level they resemble those of Fritz Lang in that the action most often occurs at night, with huge slabs of light cutting the darkness from a single source, or those of Jules Dassin in their use of thunder, lightning and rain to indicate delirious states of mind. Siodmak's themes, however, set him apart from both. His central figures are not manipulated by an ironic external fate like Lang's heroes, nor are they dreamers like those of Dassin. Most characteristically, they are driven from within by intense hatreds or loves. The network of relationships within *Christmas Holiday* (1944) is an example. A young army lieutenant is returning to the West coast with an obsessive hatred for the woman he was to have married, but who has married someone else. His plane is forced by bad weather to land in New Orleans, where he visits a brothel and ends up taking one of the girls, Jackie (Deanna Durbin), to midnight Mass. She breaks down and tells the story of her former life, in which she loved a man so completely as to be unable to perceive the faults in his character. The man, Robert (Gene Kelly), whose mother has an incestuous fixation on him, is imprisoned for murder, but escapes and comes to the brothel, hating his wife obsessively for what she has become.

It is within such an emotional register that Siodmak's characters habitually move. Philip Marshall (Charles Laughton), the middle-aged central figure of *The Suspect* (1944), kills twice in order to protect the young woman (Ella Raines) with whom he has become involved. The phantom lady in the film of that title becomes insane after the death of her lover. Ole Anderson and Steve Thompson (both played by Burt Lancaster), the central figures of *The Killers* (1946) and *Criss Cross* (1949), are destroyed by their delirious loves; and Vittorio Candella (Victor Mature), the police lieutenant in *Cry of the City* (1948), hunts his quarry, Martin Rome (Richard Conte), with an almost metaphysical hatred. Such obsessive loves and hatreds sometimes pass into psychosis. Both Terry (Olivia de Havilland), the murderous twin in *The Dark Mirror* (1946), and Marlowe (Franchot Tone), the sculptor/strangler in *The Phantom Lady* (1944), are paranoiac.

103

Siodmak's expressionism: Elisha Cook Jnr in *The Phantom Lady*; Deanna Durbin in *Christmas Holiday*; and (*opposite*) Richard Conte in *Cry of the City*

Round these figures there is a dark, hallucinatory, urban world of deserted and dangerous streets, brothels, bars and expensive apartments. Like Hitchcock in *Psycho* or Franju in *Eyes Without a Face*, Siodmak often invites his audience into this world by the use of the forward tracking shot. In the opening of *The Killers*, the point of view is from the back seat of the killers' car as it hurtles through the darkness towards the little town where Ole waits to be killed. *The Dark Mirror* opens on a black city-scape, the view of which turns out to be from an apartment window; the camera pans slowly round the room picking up a loudly ticking clock, then tracks forward to a room illuminated by an overturned light. The track stops on a large mirror in which a grotesque statue is reflected, stating visually the central theme of the film (the relationship between identical twins). The camera pans again to pick up a stabbed corpse, thus setting the plot in motion.

In the period 1944–49, Siodmak worked within the gangster film three times: *The Killers, Cry of the City* and *Criss Cross*. It is appropriate that Siodmak should have made *The Killers*, the Kafkaesque situation of a man refusing to run from his murderers being so characteristic of his world. This situation is, of course, in the Hemingway short story, but Siodmak suffuses the incident of the killing with his own style: Ole leaning on his bed, trapped like a hypnotised rabbit in the harsh shaft of light from the door kicked open by the killers (emblematically embodied in Charles McGraw and William Conrad), whose exploding guns light up their faces with every shot. The script for *The Killers* was written by John Huston (uncredited) and Anthony Veiller, and its structure (a series of flashbacks) and relationships (for example, Ole and Police Lieutenant Lubinsky were kids in the same neighbourhood) are characteristic of the genre at this time. Yet again, the flashback structure, the raking over of time and memory to reveal obsession and betrayal, seems characteristic of Siodmak. Piecing together the puzzle leading up to Ole's death is an insurance investigator, Reardon (Edmond O'Brien), who talks to the people in Ole's past. Lubinsky's wife, Ole's ex-girl, tells of the time Ole first met Kitty Collins (Ava Gardner), the woman who betrays him. Typically, in Siodmak's work and in the genre as a whole, his sexual enslavement (like that of the Elisha Cook Jnr figure in *The Phantom Lady*) is expressed in a musical context, Kitty's singing. It emerges that Kitty has induced Ole to double-cross his partners in the robbery, take all the money and go away with her. Having established his culpability in the eyes of the gang, she then deserts him with the money and marries Colfax (Albert Dekker), the leader of the gang. With an irony characteristic of Siodmak, and of Huston in this period of his work, Colfax dies before he can utter the words which will save Kitty from prison.

*The Killers* opens with two murderers hunting down and killing a man in a dark house on a dark night; *Cry of the City* begins with two policemen relentlessly pursuing a killer as he

Burt Lancaster seduced by Ava Gardner's Circe call in *The Killers*

lies, surrounded by his praying family, badly wounded in a hospital as dark and grim as a medieval keep. As they enter the hospital the wail of a police siren, a recurring sound in Siodmak's world, can be heard. As in *The Killers*, the policeman, Candella, and the killer, Rome, come from the same Italian neighbourhood, the texture of which is well evoked in Richard Murphy's script (his interest in community is also apparent in his scripts for *Boomerang* and *Panic in the Streets*). In this film, the fact that Candella and Rome are from the same neighbourhood is crucial to the central narrative – Candella's Dostoievskian pursuit of Rome, which goes far beyond the call of duty. It is clear that Candella sees in Rome what he himself might have, perhaps wants to, become. It is one of the strengths of *Cry of the City* that this fact, not presented explicitly in the script, is worked out in the *mise en scène*.

Positive and negative image: Victor Mature and Richard Conte in *Cry of the City*

Like Rome, Candella becomes a wounded fugitive from a hospital bed. Throughout the film Rome wears a white coat and Candella a black one, not in token of a facile reversal of these ancient iconographical values, but rather suggesting the positive and negative image, similarity underlying apparent opposition. (This use of the positive and negative image is repeated by Arthur Penn in depicting Billy the Kid and Pat Garret in *The Left-Handed Gun*.) The metaphysical quality of the struggle between Rome and Candella is underlined in their battle for the soul of Rome's younger brother, in the location of their final confrontation, a darkened church, and in the Langian resonance of Candella's cry to the fleeing gangster, 'Rome, in the name of the law, stop.'

Throughout the pursuit Rome leaves a trail of pain and betrayal; the ward sister, his ex-girl-friend, the unregistered emigré doctor from Europe who tends his wound, all suffer for helping Rome, as the inflexible Candella wields the law against them. In one of the most characteristic sequences of Siodmak's work, Rome seeks help from a masseuse who has been involved in the torture and death of an old lady whose jewels Rome has stolen. Rome approaches her house along a dark street and rings her bell. A tiny square of light with a figure outlined in it appears through the glass, and the figure moves forward illuminating each room in turn until she appears, massive and repellent, at the front door. There follows a scene which is strangely erotic, yet heavy with menace and potential cruelty, as Rome and the masseuse discuss a deal for his passing on the jewels to her. She induces him to relax, murmuring soft words and massaging his shoulders with enormous hands which suddenly tighten round his throat.

The physical grossness of the masseuse, her erotic brutality and the stylised way we are introduced to her, exemplify the grotesque, hallucinatory world Siodmak re-created in *Criss Cross*. This is again the story of a sexual obsessive, Steve Thompson, and the film opens in a darkened car-park with Steve kissing Anna (Yvonne de Carlo) among the flashing headlights and brutal shapes of the cars. Like *The Killers*, the story is told largely in flashbacks, one of which depicts the sexual enslavement of Steve as he watches Anna dancing to a feverish Afro-Cuban rhythm. Like Ole in *The Killers*, Steve, a payroll guard, cheats the gang who think he is with them in the robbery, intending to join Anna to whom he has given the money. As Steve lies wounded in the hospital after the robbery, Siodmak evokes his fevered condition and fear of reprisals from Slim Dundee (Dan Duryea), the leader of the gang and Anna's husband, by having him view the corridor outside his room as a reflection in a tilted mirror. The bland 'salesman' sitting in the corridor, whom Steve trusts to drive him to Anna's hideout, turns out to be in Dundee's pay. Dundee comes to the hideout – a hut set in a Dali-like landscape – after Anna has betrayed Steve and is gathering together the money to leave. Dundee leaves them dead in each other's arms, and the

Genre and title reaffirmed: the end for a gangster in *Cry of the City* ▶

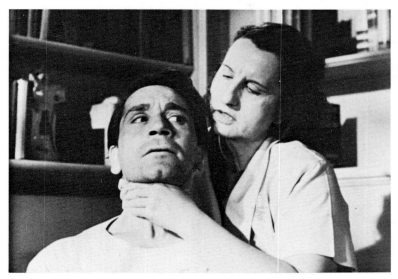

Erotic brutality: gangster and masseuse in *Cry of the City* (Richard Conte, Hope Emerson)

film ends with the wail of the police siren which sounded over Martin Rome's dead body in *Cry of the City*.

Darkness, cruelty, obsession, betrayal and death are the hall-marks of Siodmak's work. It is fitting that the theme music of *Christmas Holiday* should be 'Always' and of *Cry of the City*, 'Never'. These are the emotional polarities of Siodmak's world.

# 9: Elia Kazan

'I know I shall be washed clean in America.'
Stavros in *The Anatolian Smile*

In 1962, after a distinguished career in the theatre and in the cinema, Elia Kazan published his first literary work, a semi-autobiographical novel entitled *America, America*. It is the story of a poor Anatolian Greek boy who, despite harrowing experiences of poverty, treachery and violence, retains his dream of America and eventually lands there as an immigrant. However, the dream is corroded almost as soon as he lands as he witnesses the bribing of an immigration official. It is paradoxical that this explicit confrontation with America should come after what seemed to be the end of Kazan's cinematic career; for concern with the forging of America by twentieth-century events and critical appraisal of American values seem, in retrospect, to form a dominant motif, perhaps *the* dominant motif, of his film work. That this is so is due in some measure to the mood of the period when his directorial career in the cinema began.

He began directing feature films in 1945, and throughout the Forties worked mainly with 20th Century-Fox who, under Darryl F. Zanuck, were producing a kind of sub-genre called the social exposé which often, though by no means invariably, overlapped with the gangster film. Thus Kazan, in common with many young directors in the post-war, pre-McCarthy period, confronted in his films some of the grosser evils of American society: anti-Semitism in *Gentleman's Agreement*

(1947), anti-Negro feeling in *Pinky* (1949). During the period of the HUAC hearings and the blacklist, Kazan earned the vilification of some left-wing critics for explicitly dissociating himself from his former Communist Party colleagues (he had been a member from 1934 to 1936). His only completely political film, *Viva Zapata!* (1952), has been widely read as an anti-communist tract, but it is perhaps truer to say that it is anti-ideological, the intellectual theorist of the Revolution, Aguirre, being presented in very harsh terms. Kazan's scepticism about the usefulness of intellectuals is also apparent in his *A Face in the Crowd* (1957). However, Kazan again weighed America in the balance in a remarkable group of films which he produced as well as directed: *East of Eden* (1955), *Wild River* (1960) and *Splendour in the Grass* (1961) – and of course the film of his own novel *America, America* (*The Anatolian Smile*, 1964). *A Face in the Crowd*, though of the same period as these films, is, in its barefaced confrontation of the misuse of the power of television, closer in mood to the social exposé films of the late Forties.

In *East of Eden*, *Wild River* and *Splendour in the Grass*, Kazan deals with three of the major watersheds in twentieth-century American history, respectively the First World War, the New Deal and the Wall Street Crash of 1929. It should be said that there is another major motif in Kazan's work, one that often pulls him away from his wider social concerns: this is his interest in intense, almost abnormal, psychological situations. This interest probably derives from his work in the theatre and, in particular, from his association with the Actors' Studio (of which he was co-founder in 1948) and his successful staging of the work of Thornton Wilder, Arthur Miller, Tennessee Williams and others. It has often drawn him to baroque players such as Marlon Brando, James Dean, Lee J. Cobb and Karl Malden. So intense is the examination of the psychological situation in *East of Eden* that the First World War recedes and becomes little more than background material, although there is a strong sense of the Puritan oversimplification of American

114

*mores*, the artificial polarisation of good and evil, destroying young lives and forcing the local citizenry to an extreme anti-German position.

The social and psychological themes are much better integrated in *Splendour in the Grass*, in which the Calvinist sexual *mores* of rural America, which drive young people to despair and madness, seem but another facet of the intense acquisitiveness resulting in the Wall Street Crash of 1929. In *Wild River* the social theme, which is presented with a subtle irony characteristic of Kazan's later work, is that of American progress versus American individualism. The psychological theme, a girl from the Tennessee Valley rejecting the despair of her widowhood and marrying the representative of the New Deal, is clearly better integrated here than in *East of Eden*, but the overall impression is of the predominance of the social theme. As Ella Garth's house, symbol of the old order, goes up in flames, it is counterpointed in the frame by the Stars and Stripes fluttering from the mast of the boat that will take her off her island. The final image of the film is of the dam which will flood the Tennessee Valley, an image giving almost mystical endorsement to the New Deal.

Elia Kazan has worked within the gangster film/thriller on three occasions: in *Boomerang* (1947), *Panic in the Streets* (1950) and *On the Waterfront* (1954). *Boomerang*, made for 20th Century-Fox and produced by Louis de Rochemont, bears several marks of the location thriller associated with his name. The image behind the credits is of a police file, suggesting the documentary nature of what is to follow. The characters and locale, a small town in Connecticut, are announced by commentary; the location thriller's interest in the technology of detection is apparent in the details of making identikit pictures. As the commentary puts it, 'the quiet pool of community life is stirred up' by the shooting of a well-loved citizen, Father Lambert. There is strong local feeling against the police department and City Hall for failing to make an arrest, and the reform party, coming up for re-election, put pressure on their

Scientific detection: Dana Andrews in *Boomerang*

State's Attorney, Henry Harvey (Dana Andrews), to secure an arrest and conviction, while the opposing party (machine politicians) make political capital out of his failure to do so. When an arrest is made and a trial mounted, Harvey, though technically the prosecutor, presents evidence which demonstrates the innocence of the arrested man.

The most obvious Kazan elements here are the interest in the complex pressures within a community and in the nature of the hero. The shortcomings of the structure of American city politics are immediately apparent, for it is because the Police Chief and State's Attorney are political nominees that City Hall can put pressure on them to pervert the course of Justice. Newspapermen in American films have in general been regarded as defenders of democracy and the public right to know; in *Boomerang* their presentation is more complex. The reporter, Woods (Sam Levene), is in the American muckraking tradition, and it is he who, in a typically Kazanian rejection of

116

*Boomerang*: the community versus the outsider (Karl Malden, Arthur Kennedy); (*below*) muckraking reporter exposes corrupt politician (Sam Levene, Ed Begley)

oversimplification, exposes the corruption in the reform party, while working for a paper controlled by the machine politicians. The Police Chief, Robinson (Lee J. Cobb), consistently rejects the muscle of his subordinates in obtaining confessions, yet he is aware that his own method, prolonged questioning until the prisoner gives up and confesses to anything, is different only in degree. As he carries the exhausted prisoner Waldron (Arthur Kennedy) to his bed, he mutters with self-disgust, 'What a way to earn a living.' The inhabitants of the community, law-abiding citizens normally, are ready to form a lynch mob (like the citizens in *East of Eden*) on the basis of an arrest.

The character and dilemma of Henry Harvey obviously interested Kazan, for he was to return to them in some of his later work. Harvey is virtually offered the state governorship to secure a conviction against Waldron, but he chooses to act on principle rather than self-interest, to follow the direction of the evidence and establish Waldron's innocence. Kazan's interest both in community and in the individualist hero is summed up in Harvey's conversation with his political boss McCreery (Robert Keith) about whether the life of one man is more important than the stability and progress of a community.

It would be absurd to claim that *Boomerang* was, for Kazan, a completely personal film or that it is, even within its own terms, a total success. Among the more obvious weaknesses is the undeveloped character of Lambert's assassin, who appears on the fringes of the main action and is finally killed in a car crash, and the extreme theatricality of Harvey's demonstration, with a loaded gun in court, of Waldron's innocence. It seems reasonable to describe *Boomerang* as a competent exercise in genre film-making which reflects some of its author's abiding thematic interests.

*Panic in the Streets*, also produced by 20th Century-Fox, came at the end of the cycle of location thrillers. In one sense the New Orleans waterfront locales are a mannerism of the genre; in another, the locale allows Kazan to examine the texture of the immigrant Armenian community and its implacable suspicion of the wider American community (its refusal to co-operate with the police and public health authorities; its unwillingness to have its own sick removed to a hospital outside the district). But the purely immigrant elements of the film are secondary to the main situation and the character of the hero, both recognisably Kazanian. An immigrant Armenian is murdered, but the public health authorities discover that he is carrying pneumonic plague. There follows a desperate search to track down and immunise all who were in contact with the carrier, with, in the background, the imminent threat of the complete disruption of the community by panic. This develops finally into a chase of the men who murdered the plague carrier. The central figure, Clint Reed (Richard Widmark), is a doctor in the public health service who, like Henry Harvey, has to fight official obstruction, initially from the police department, to follow a course of action which he believes to be right.

Genre cinema functions primarily in its physical action rather than in its exploration of character or situation. Kazan handles the conventions of the genre, such as the initial killing of the plague carrier and the final chase of his assailants, with the strong dramatic sense, in terms of movement of actors and timing of violence, which characterises his work as a whole. The swift conventions of action are fleshed out by Kazan's obvious interest in the characters, who have a physical and emotional individuality (Jack Palance as the controlled psychopath, Blackie; Zero Mostel as the vacillating sidekick, Fitch) not always associated with genre cinema.

Indeed, Kazan poses a problem for the critic taking a genre perspective. One can sense that the films of, say, Don Siegel, would be very little different if the tradition of the gangster movie had never existed, in the sense that the genre's recurrent iconography and themes seem very close to the images required to express Siegel's view of the world. Kazan, however, is a very different artist from Siegel, both in his themes and in the lack of directness in his *mise en scène*. Where Siegel's *mise en scène* works by broad strokes and a narrow repertoire of gestures, Kazan's works by nuance, subtlety and an extraordinarily wide range of gesture and movement from his actors. Where Siegel seldom gives the feeling of reaching towards a meaning wider than that contained in the image, Kazan is habitually creating images with resonances beyond themselves. For example, the final chase of Blackie in *Panic in the Streets* is handled very much in a traditional genre way, forcefully and competently. However, Blackie's last attempt at escape is by climbing the hawser by which a ship is moored to the quay. When he reaches the large metal disc placed on the hawser to prevent rats boarding the ship, he cannot pass it and falls into the water. The resonance of this image suggests that a study of Kazan's *mise en scène* might go some way to revealing the nature of his art. For instance, the fact that he repeatedly builds scenes of violence round automobiles (the execution of Madero in *Viva Zapata!*, the attempted rape in *Pinky*, the collective rape of Ginny in *Splendour in the Grass*, the attack on Chuck Glover in *Wild River*) may be related to an early association of automobiles with violence. In Kazan's partly autobiographical novel *The Arrangement* the hero describes his father hitting his mother:

He looked at her a long time, his eyes glaring, his eyebrows stiff as bone, his face full of blood like a sponge. Then he hit her, open palm across the side of her face, and knocked her to the floor ... I remember all through this the sound of an automobile horn outside.

This passage may also throw light on the scene in *On the Waterfront* where Terry tells the girl about his involvement in her brother's murder, and the scene in *The Anatolian Smile* in which Stavros murders the Turk.

*On the Waterfront* would not immediately be described as a gangster film. Yet the movie deals with that area of overlap between crime and union activity which was common in the gangster films of the late Thirties, its action is expressed through an immigrant Catholic community, the Irish

120

Images with resonances beyond themselves: the doomed escape in *Panic in the Streets* (Jack Palance, Richard Widmark)

longshoremen of the New York waterfront, and it handles the iconography of the genre, especially cars and figures, with great facility. It perhaps goes further than is permissible in purely genre films (if such exist) in the exploration and individuality of its characters. Its central figure, Terry Molloy (Marlon Brando), a badly marked, inarticulate ex-boxer, is a very different man from the articulate lawyer Henry Harvey of *Boomerang*. But he faces precisely the same dilemma, whether to remain silent and thus maintain the security of his friends, or speak the truth and accept the consequences to his own self-interest. Terry's motives for speaking the truth are actually more complex than Harvey's: he testifies before the Waterfront Crime Commission, thus breaking the power of the corrupt union boss Johnny Friendly, partly out of principle, partly because he is attracted to the sister of a man killed by Friendly's hoods, and partly out of revenge for Friendly's having killed his brother. Harvey, by contrast, acts purely out of principle. It is part of the character of Terry Molloy that he is not fully aware of the complexity of his motives. Kazan's interest in character is further apparent in the solidity and intensity of the rendering of Father Barry (Karl Malden) and Johnny Friendly (Lee J. Cobb), both played by actors with whom he had worked in the theatre.

*On the Waterfront*, especially its closing sequence in which Terry Molloy rises from a severe beating by Friendly's hoods to lead the longshoremen back to work, has been attacked by several critics, most notably Lindsay Anderson, on the grounds that whereas the script makes several explicit references to collective action, the last sequence does not bear this out and is, in mood, élitist rather than egalitarian. If in absolute terms (by comparison with, say, some of Eisenstein's films) this is so, it is well to remember that the American ethic is individualistic, that Kazan's own ethic (to judge from *America, America*) is, or has been, individualistic, that his heroes are consistently individualistic, and that the traditions of dénouement within the gangster genre are individualistic. To expect Kazan to make a

The price of controlling the waterfront. Lee J. Cobb displays his 'war wounds' for Marlon Brando in *On the Waterfront*

collectivist film, and then to brand him fascist when he does not, seems disingenuous.

Despite the richness of his *mise en scène*, Elia Kazan is not one of the great formal innovators of the cinema. Indeed, his work suggests that his approach to cinema is by way of ideas, characters and dramatised situations rather than by awareness of formal properties. Thus the interest in his films resides in the consistency of his thematic concerns, the psychological intensity of his characters, and the dramatic intensity of incidents. His achievement in this respect is far from negligible.

# 10: Nicholas Ray

'. . . I have one working title: *I'm a Stranger Here Myself.'*
Nicholas Ray

If there is a single image which sums up Nicholas Ray's view of the human condition, it is that of the hunt. Sometimes this is expressed in terms of man and the animal world (*Wind Across the Everglades, The Savage Innocents*), but more usually in terms of man hunting his own kind (*They Live By Night, On Dangerous Ground* and, vestigially, *Johnny Guitar* and *The James Brothers*). Where other directors have consistently explored the figure of the predator, Ray's interest and sympathy have been, more often, with the prey. Ray's people are insecure, unstable, scarred by their surroundings or carrying within themselves the seeds of their own destruction. His heroes are often young, confused and vulnerable (*They Live By Night, Knock On Any Door, Rebel Without a Cause, The James Brothers*), or bear outward signs of emotional isolation (Tommy Farrell's game leg in *Party Girl*, Mary Walden's blindness in *On Dangerous Ground*). They may reject progress and modernity; they may choose to go or are sent into primitive areas (the desert in *Bitter Victory*, the Florida swamps in *Wind Across the Everglades*, rural New England in *On Dangerous Ground*). The journeys which bring them closer to nature may also offer them hope of salvation.

A description of Nicholas Ray's themes, involving, as it must, words such as 'alienation', 'loneliness' and 'insecurity', seems to place him solidly in the mainstream of twentieth-century art. The words give little insight into the uniqueness of Ray's work. Ray is an articulate critic of his own films, but he seems more at ease discussing character and theme than evaluating the *mise en scène* which carries their impact. Indeed, his attempts to discuss *mise en scène* are often evasive and sometimes banal, as when he describes the helicopter shots in *They Live By Night* as representing 'the long arm of fate, doom'. Yet in so far as theme and *mise en scène* are separable, it is the complexity and frequent violence of the latter which makes the experience of watching a Nicholas Ray movie so unique.

Victor Perkins, in an excellent essay on Ray in *Movie 9*, describes the *completeness* of Ray's *mise en scène*, how meaning is invariably carried not simply in one or two dimensions but in all the elements in the total experience: script, actors, locale, décor, time of day, sound, lighting, colour and montage, all working to the same end. The particular turbulence of Ray's *mise en scène* can most accurately be communicated by describing how he mounts scenes of violence. The audience is rarely a passive observer, but more usually a participant, the violence sometimes coming from the characters into the camera (as in Jim Wilson's beating-up of Bernie Tucker in *On Dangerous Ground*, Chickamaw's crowbar swipe at Bowie in *They Live By Night*, and Rico's attack on Frankie with a miniature silver billiard cue in *Party Girl*). In none of these cases does the violence come *directly* into the camera as it would if the camera were representing the subjective position of one of the characters: it seems to be directed, more disturbingly, at an area behind the camera – in terms of the viewing experience, at us, the audience. Alternatively, Ray sometimes reverses the process, so that acts of violence seem to be perpetrated by the audience on his characters (as with the slash of the ex-jockey's riding crop across Beef's face in *Wind Across the Everglades*, and the precisely similar scenes in *The James Brothers* and *Party Girl* in which figures moving at speed towards the camera are shot down by guns which suddenly appear in the left of the frame).

Audience as perpetrator of violence: *On Dangerous Ground* (Robert Ryan, Richard Irving)

This turbulence extends to other elements of his *mise en scène*, for example through the powerful, primitive images of fire which recur in his work. One such image is worth discussing in detail, for it involves several of Ray's particular skills. In *Johnny Guitar*, when Vienna is arrested and led out of her saloon, Emma returns with a shotgun and shoots through the rope holding the chandelier, which crashes to the floor setting the place alight. Emma watches the blaze with outstretched hands, and backs out of the door. A cut to the outside of the saloon shows the flames licking through the boards as Emma, raven-haired and wearing a black dress, backs towards the camera. As she looms into it she turns sharply to show her face contorted with the ecstasy of destruction. It is one of the most visceral moments in the cinema, achieved by Ray's sense of dress and décor, his awareness of the power of primitive imagery and his skill in the handling and placing both of actors and the camera. The vigorous image of the burning automobile in *They Live By Night* is echoed in the work of other directors with baroque sensibilities, most notably Roman Polanski and Arthur Penn.

Few directors have produced such a personal and accomplished first film as *They Live By Night*. The central figures, Bowie (Farley Granger) and Keechie (Cathy O'Donnell), are already familiar Ray creations, scarred, suspicious and directionless (ironically, the theme music is 'I Know Where I'm Going'). The dialogue is resonant with animal imagery: Keechie's father describes her as a dog and a weasel and Bowie's movements behind the billboards and in the shed at the beginning of the film are reminiscent of a hunted animal. Keechie and Bowie overcome their initial suspicion and hostility; each sensing the other's isolation, together they seek to become, as they put it, 'like real people'. It emerges in the dialogue that Keechie's mother has deserted her and that Bowie's mother married the man who killed his father in a pool-room brawl; but their inability to be 'like real people' is presented more subtly. At the first sight of Keechie her sex is indeterminate; and Bowie, having expressed amazement that Mattie (the embittered gangster's wife who gives them shelter) lives 'in a real house', proceeds to draw the plan of a robbery on her cushions.

Like Jesse and Zee in *The James Brothers*, Keechie and Bowie try to isolate his violent life of robbery from their life together by going to live in a remote cabin. Bowie's gift to Keechie of a watch, which she is unable to set because there are no clocks around, carries suggestions both of an attempt to make time stand still and the inevitability of their time together running out. Until the end of the film, in which Bowie is shot down by the police, the police are hunting him, but this danger seems remote. The real threat to the private world created by Bowie and Keechie is Chickamaw (Howard da Silva), whose grotesque fish-eye acts as a visual shorthand for his brutality and evil. He often carries implements with violent connotations,

*They Live By Night*: (*above*) overtones of classical tragedy (Cathy O'Donnell, Helen Craig); (*below*) the threat to a private world (Farley Granger, Howard da Silva)

a shotgun or a razor, and the potentially directionless quality of his savagery is shown by his irrational breaking of a mirror in his quarrel with Mattie. Ray indicates the threat he poses to Bowie and Keechie's private world, and also the precariousness of that world, in the single image of Chickamaw tinkering with and smashing the baubles on Keechie's Christmas tree. However, Chickamaw is killed before the end of the film and the principal agent of Bowie's destruction becomes Mattie. It is clear in retrospect that Mattie is conceived as a figure of doom. While her ashen face and funereal clothes serve to indicate her isolation and virtual widowhood (her husband is in jail), they also carry overtones of death figures in classical tragedy.

Where the central figures of *They Live By Night* are hunted, the hero of *On Dangerous Ground*, Jim Wilson (Robert Ryan), is a predator. Nicholas Ray has described him as 'a man whose job is that of a member of a violence squad whose job is to apprehend or to prevent violence and yet who has that same violence within him.'\* The opening of the film is constructed to demonstrate Wilson's isolation. Pete Santos, Bill Daly and Wilson, the police anti-violence team, are all shown in their domestic contexts before going out on patrol. Pete's wife straps on his pistol, kisses him and says how she hates being left alone; Bill is surrounded by a brood of children; but Wilson is alone, studying pictures of wanted criminals as he eats his meal. It becomes clear that in many ways Wilson is a model policeman. Checking over a bar, he has a juvenile evicted and refuses a bribe; but his capacity for violence becomes apparent when his colleagues have to restrain him from assaulting a citizen who expresses his low opinion of the police for stopping and searching him. Wilson's willingness to use his attractiveness to get information from a girl, and thereby put her in danger as a stool-pigeon, causes Pete to observe that he values

---

\* This seems to be a theme with which Ray was preoccupied at this time, magnificently realised in *In a Lonely Place* (1949).

people lightly. Following the severe beating he gives a suspect, and his maniacal assault on the attacker of the girl who gave him the information, the cause and the cure of his violence are made explicit in an exchange with Bill Daly:

*Wilson:* Garbage! That's all we handle, garbage! How do you live with it?
*Daly:* I don't live with it, I live with other people.

To cool the situation resulting from his beating up of the suspect, Wilson is sent from the city to a remote part of the state (which he calls Siberia) to assist in the detection of a sex murderer. Ray shows the journey by a series of tracking shots from the front seat of a car, each shot dissolving into the next to give a cumulative effect of remoteness and placidity in marked contrast to the previous scenes in the city. The snow-scapes of this film point forward to those of *The Savage Innocents*. As is true of other Ray heroes, Jim Wilson's return to nature is an occasion for increased self-knowledge and implied salvation. He is forced to confront vicariously the violent elements in his own nature in the shape of Walter Brent (Ward Bond), the berserk father of the murdered girl.

It emerges that the murderer is a half-witted boy, Danny Walden, and after two hunting sequences of enormous excitement and brutality (achieved by the animal imagery of Danny leaping from a tree, his pursuers following his tracks in the snow, and the violent insistence of Bernard Herrmann's score), Brent and Wilson track him to the house where he lives with his blind sister, Mary (Ida Lupino). Mary is saved from the total isolation of Jim Wilson by her devotion to and care of her brother. Their situation is presented as idyllic, the name Walden recalls Thoreau's natural paradise, and Mary even has a tree in her living-room. The metaphor of Danny as prey, implied in the stalking sequences, becomes more explicit in his animal-like movements, his whimpering, and in the den (the typical private world of Ray's people) he has made for himself full of wood-carvings of animals. The Waldens' world has a

*On Dangerous Ground*: (*above*) the tree in the living-room (Robert Ryan, Ida Lupino); (*below*) animal imagery and the hunted boy (Sumner Williams)

131

humanising effect on Jim Wilson, and he conquers the violence within himself by trying to contain the violence of Brent. Interestingly, after Danny has fallen to his death from a cliff and Brent, purged of his fury, has uttered a phrase recurrent in Ray's work, 'He's just a boy,' Mary's new isolation and lack of purpose is indicated by her knocking over and breaking the objects in her living-room, like Keechie's smashing of the domestic pottery with Bowie's gun. Ray wanted to end the film on the ambivalent image of Jim Wilson returning to the bleak city, but as the film now stands, he goes back once more to Mary Walden.

Ray was to return to the theme of scarred and mutually hostile people being humanised by loving each other in *Party Girl* (1958), one of the late Fifties cycle of gangster films in which the Twenties and Thirties were reconstructed. Vicki Gaye (Cyd Charisse), a night-club dancer, and Tommy Farrell (Robert Taylor), a legal mouthpiece for the mobs, are both sexually alienated, she by an unpleasant experience in her adolescence, he by being driven from his wife's bed by her disgust at his game leg. The growth of their relationship from mutual insults to sexual tenderness is interwoven with Ray's extreme sensitivity to two aspects of the gangster film: its sexuality and its violence. The central relationship is threatened by both these aspects of the gangsters' world. The musical sequence backing the credits, in which Vicki is a member of the chorus, turns out to be a meat display at which Louis Canetto (John Ireland) chooses the best cuts for the party to be given by Rico Angelo (Lee J. Cobb), who controls crime in the city. The idea of sex as a commodity is restated at the party when the chorus girls are paid as they enter.

Ray's handling of violence in *Party Girl* is reminiscent of *The Big Heat*, in the way it poses the threat of violence to women. Much of the violence is by implication or by proxy, as when Rico fires several bullets through a photograph of Jean Harlow, or invites Tommy Farrell to consider what a crow-bar swipe could do to his recently healed leg. The two most

*Party Girl*: the 'meat parade' credit sequence (Cyd Charisse at centre)

horrifying possibilities of violence, one realised, the other only potential, occur in the same locale, a dingy club-room beside a railway. In the first, Rico attends a dinner, ostensibly to present a miniature silver billiard-cue to a long-serving lieutenant. The passing trains evoke a mounting sense of imminent violence (as in Bowie's death-scene in *They Live By Night*) as Rico's eulogy becomes a tirade and he clubs his lieutenant into insensibility with the cue. This act of violence at a gangsters' dinner obviously has resonances in the genre (see *The St Valentine's Day Massacre* and *Some Like It Hot*), but in the context of *Party Girl* it is present primarily to give added force to a very complex scene later in the film.

Tommy Farrell has decided to turn state's evidence against Rico, who then seizes Vicki as hostage and has Tommy brought to the same club-room by the railway where he is holding her. He there produces a bottle of acid and invites

Tommy to consider what it could do to Vicki's face. Vicki is then brought in wearing a brilliant red dress and with her face bandaged. The bandages are slowly unwrapped to reveal that her face is still intact. The locale becomes extremely important at this point, for as the trains rattle past the audience recalls the association of trains with violence in the earlier scene. But even more important in this scene of violence by proxy is the effect Ray obtains by colour symbolism. Early in the film Vicki has worn the same red dress; which at that stage appears to be a fairly traditional visual shorthand for the life she leads, especially since, as her relationship with Tommy develops, she is seen in soft browns, tans and black. However, the reappearance of her red dress in the final sequence causes the audience to extend its earlier reading and see Ray's colour symbolism as, in the clearest sense, red for danger, the danger to Vicki – in sexual terms early in the film, in terms of violence at the end – of her proximity to the gangsters. Ray brilliantly uses the colour of Vicki's dress to suggest, indirectly, what the acid could do to her by having Rico pour some of it on to a Christmas bell precisely the same colour as the dress.

The reappearance of the red dress in the final sequence of the film thus serves several ends, one of which is to act as a reminder of Vicki's earlier life and to counterpoint it with the tender relationship she now has with Tommy. The former inadequacy of Tommy's own life is similarly recapitulated in the final sequence. Earlier in the film Tommy had evoked the jury's pity during a courtroom sequence by limping more than usual, and, especially, by focusing their attention on a watch which he claimed had been given him by his father. These tricks were used to secure an acquittal on a murder charge for the guilty Louis Canetto. In the final sequence Tommy purges his own past by again using the trick with the watch, but this time to delay Rico's act of violence against Vicki until the police arrive. *Party Girl* is an unusual film for Ray in that both central characters escape from their pasts; and, at the close of the film, they have at least the possibility of a future together.

◀ *Party Girl*: violence realised (Lee J. Cobb and ambitious employee) and violence by proxy (the shot-up photograph of Jean Harlow, and John Ireland and Robert Taylor with the acid bottle marked for Cyd Charisse)

It is one of the tragedies of the commercial cinema that it could not accommodate Nicholas Ray. The commercial failure of *King of Kings* and *Fifty-Five Days at Peking*, two epic exercises in themselves uncharacteristic of Ray, was no doubt a factor in his withdrawal from Hollywood. Ray now moves between Europe and the United States, tinkering with low-budget, near-underground projects but still showing his inventive talent in the experiments he has conducted with split screens and multiple images. His early return to the commercial cinema is earnestly to be hoped for, though hardly to be expected.

# 11: Samuel Fuller

There are, in Samuel Fuller's experience and sensibility, three elements which determine the nature of his work: his early career as a crime reporter and pulp novelist, his service as an infantryman in North Africa and Europe during the Second World War, and his intense feeling about America. The first two of these go some way towards explaining why he habitually expresses himself through violent genres such as the Western, the gangster film and the war movie. But irrespective of the genres within which he works, his films display a striking thematic continuity, the core of which is the question of national loyalty.

Thus a gangster film such as *Pickup on South Street*, a Western such as *Run of the Arrow*, and a war movie such as *China Gate*, all have central figures forced to make decisions about their national allegiances; or more correctly, who adopt courses of action by which these allegiances are determined. But allegiance to one nation only is conceivable in Fuller's world, and that nation is America. This leads to inconsistencies in his work. In the film most explicitly concerned with national loyalty, *Run of the Arrow*, a Southerner, O'Meara (Rod Steiger), refusing to live under the Union flag after Lee's surrender, goes West and joins the Sioux nation. The Sioux capture a brutal and callous Union officer (Ralph Meeker) and according to their tribal traditions, proceed to torture him to death. O'Meara, in an act of mercy, shoots him, thereby demonstrating his instinctive loyalties. He leaves the Sioux nation and returns to the Union. On the surface, this would appear to be a racial rather than a national choice, but the lack of consistency with Fuller's other work indicates that to Fuller the source of transcendental value is the nation rather than the race. For example, in *Hell and High Water*, a sympathetic Chinese communist appeals to an American Chinese for information, but the latter chooses America and betrays him. Also, in *Crimson Kimono*, one suspects that the decision of Christine to marry the civilised Nisei rather than his white friend is endorsed by the director. The anti-crime forces in *Underworld USA* include a Nisei, a Negro and a Puerto Rican. Fuller's mystical America subsumes racial loyalties.

Fuller has worked within the gangster film on three occasions: *Pickup on South Street* (1953), *House of Bamboo* (1955) and *Underworld USA* (1960). He has worked once in the related sub-genre of the *film policier*: *The Crimson Kimono* (1959). *Pickup on South Street* appeared at the height of Senator McCarthy's power and was dismissed by critics in Britain as a McCarthyist tract. While it is, indeed, an anti-communist film, it is much less opportunistically so than these critics would allow. The original story by Dwight Taylor involved drug trafficking; Fuller's scenario changes this to microfilm which a communist organisation is trying to smuggle out of the United States. It is perfectly consistent with Fuller's attitude to America that he should view communists as the natural enemy of all America stands for, especially so in the Cold War atmosphere of the early Fifties. This is substantially the statement of *Steel Helmet* and *Fixed Bayonets* (both about the war in Korea) and *China Gate* (about the French/Viet Minh struggle in Vietnam).

Paradoxically, bourgeois America is often defended in Fuller's films by the pariahs of American society; in his war movies, psychotic mercenaries go from one war to another, ignorant of the ideological struggle they are engaged in. This is true also of *Pickup on South Street*, in which the most violent denunciations of communism come from Moe and Candy, the one a down-and-out, the other an ex-prostitute, neither of them with a stake in bourgeois America. Moe (Thelma Ritter) sells Skip (Richard Widmark) both to the police and to Candy, but refuses to sell him to the communists: 'Even in our crummy kind of business you gotta draw the line somewhere.' Throughout the film, Skip derides appeals to his national loyalty which he dismisses as 'patriotic eyewash', and when he finally brings down the communist organisation it is not because of abstract conceptions of loyalty to America but out of personal vengeance for the beating and wounding of Candy. If *Pickup* is no more than a right-wing tract, Fuller has chosen a strange hero and odd mouthpieces for his message.

The political elements in *Pickup* are confined almost solely to the dialogue.* For *Pickup* is, iconographically, a gangster film. The casting of Richard Widmark, along with Richard Conte and Victor Mature the dominant figure of the genre in the post-war period, helps to establish this, as does Fuller's version of Jean Peters: cheap, provocatively sensual and very much in the tradition of Lizabeth Scott and Marie Windsor in gangster films and thrillers of the post-war period. The milieux within which the action takes place – urban streets and subways, waterfront streets, precinct stations and lavish apartments – place the film solidly within the genre, and the presentation of the communist organisation identifies *Pickup* as a Fifties gangster film. The members of the organisation are iconographically indistinguishable from gangsters in other 'syndicate' movies of the Fifties: Joey, who is conceived and played as a hood; the cigar-smoking executive in charge of 'Security'. Only Joey's immediate superior, with the cigarette holder and tweeds which place him in the bourgeois intelligentsia, looks as if he might conceivably be part of an ideologically

---

* The dubbed version of *Pickup on South Street* released in France substituted drugs for the microfilm, so eliminating the political content.

committed organisation. As a serious political comment, *Pickup on South Street* is plainly a non-starter.

Undoubtedly, Fuller's experience as a crime reporter gives an authenticity and bleakness to the petty criminal world of *Pickup*, the qualities of which he conveys most vividly in the image of Moe's body (referred to as 'number 11') being taken by boat through the darkness to a pauper's grave.

If *Pickup on South Street* offers the paradox of the political film which is at heart a gangster film, *House of Bamboo* offers the paradox of the gangster film which is, more centrally, about war. The pre-credit sequence is, in fact, a military engagement, a robbery on an army munitions train guarded by American and Japanese soldiers. Typically in Fuller's work, the engagement is not frontal; the attackers, dressed as civilians, adopt guerrilla tactics and dispose of the guards with strangling chains. Crucially, the only fatal casualty is an American sergeant. The main opposition to the criminals therefore comes not from the Japanese police but from the American Army, and by extension, America itself. Sandy (Robert Ryan), the organiser of the robbery, has gathered round him men discharged with ignominy from the U.S. Army, and made them into a para-military unit. His briefing before a robbery, complete with maps and photographs, is conducted in military terms ('touchdown', 'objective', 'attack', 'terrain'). The gang dons naval jackets for this operation, and wounded 'casualties' are shot lest they betray the other gang members.

Fuller has described war as 'organised lunacy', and the figure of Sandy represents his most sustained critique of the military power psychosis. Forever stressing the qualities of control and decisiveness, Sandy is consistently wrong in his decisions: his breaking of his own rules by saving Spanier (Robert Stack) when he is wounded during the raid on the cement works; his deduction that Griff (Cameron Mitchell) is the informer (having characteristically diagnosed Griff's condition as 'battle fatigue'); his assumption that Mariko (Shirley Yamaguchi) goes to the Imperial Hotel to see a boy friend

'... like a five-star general': Sandy (Robert Ryan) briefs his men in *House of Bamboo*

rather than, as she does, to pass information to Captain Hanson (Brad Dexter); his ill-managed attempt to have Spanier shot by the police in the jewellery store. There are indications that under the cool exterior of the 'five-star general', Sandy is a psychotic. The truth of Spanier's remark to him that 'a strait-jacket would fit you just fine' is demonstrated in the final gun battle in which he pointlessly directs his fire into the crowded street, killing a woman.

It might be thought that Spanier's betrayal and exceptionally remorseless killing of the man who befriended him and saved his life argues a curious coldness in him; and so it would seem if his motivation were seen simply as that of the policeman chasing the criminal. But his motivation, for Fuller, goes deeper than this. Both Sandy and his newspaperman informer stress that the Army will never forgive the killing of 'one of their own'. When Spanier, without a backward glance, leaves Sandy's body in orbit on a children's merry-go-round, his act must be seen in the context of the killing of the sergeant in the pre-credit sequence, the threat this poses for the American Army and, ultimately, for America itself. The main impulse of the film therefore implicitly carries the recurrent theme of national loyalty. It appears explicitly in the relationship between Spanier and Mariko.

Unlike many of Fuller's heroines, Mariko is not a former prostitute seeking a better life. She is in many ways more courageous, taking on, in the eyes of her community, the role of the Japanese equivalent of the prostitute, the kimono girl, in order to assist Spanier. Her refinement is indicated by her keeping the nape of her neck covered by her hair (unlike the genuine kimono girls), by her horrified reaction at Sandy's party when the kimono girls change from a demure Japanese dance to a wild American jive, and by her lowering of the lattice screen between Spanier's mattress and her own. This image is complex and meaningful, encapsulating the several barriers, sexual, moral, cultural, which exist between her and Spanier. But, like other Fuller characters, she too chooses America, not out of abstract loyalty, but initially out of revenge for the death of her American husband and, eventually, out of love for Spanier.

The idea of national identity is explicitly at the centre of Fuller's later film, *The Crimson Kimono*. Charlie Bancroft (Glenn Corbett) and Joe Kojaku (James Shigeta) met 'in a foxhole in Korea', their friendship being forged in defence of America against the great menace, communism. As police officers, they work as a team and even share an apartment. Crucially, the apparent racial hatred between the two caused by their both falling in love with Chris (Victoria Shaw) provokes in Joe a crisis of *national* identity: 'What am I, American Japanese, Japanese American, Nisei? What label do I live under?' Filled with doubt, Joe decides to turn in his badge and, quitting the Caucasian world, he returns to Little Tokyo, the Japanese quarter of Los Angeles.

This theme of national identity and the narrative thrust of the film, the tracking down of the killer of the burlesque dancer Sugar Torch, are in almost Shakespearean symmetry. Roma, the killer, who makes Japanese dolls and therefore herself straddles two national cultures, has killed Sugar Torch out of fear that the burlesque dancer had stolen her lover. Dying in Joe's arms, Roma tells him that she misread her lover's attitude to Sugar Torch because of her own intense jealousy. And Joe realises that he himself misread the look on Charlie's face for racial disgust when it was in fact 'plain, honest, down to earth hatred'. Although his friendship with Charlie has been destroyed, for Fuller this is secondary, since Joe has returned from the ghetto, to become once again part of America, the rightful role of a Nisei. Fuller celebrates this role in the sequence in the Nisei military cemetery, drawing our attention to the tributes of Dwight Eisenhower and Mark Clark to the bravery and loyalty of the Nisei troops, and to the grave of one Nisei, posthumously awarded the Congressional Medal of Honor in — for Fuller — America's great contemporary Armageddon, Korea.

*The Crimson Kimono* is perhaps the most useful film within which to consider the question of Fuller's style, for it is one of his most uneven works, containing some sequences as brilliantly realised as anything he has done and others among his weakest. In each case, the success or failure is directly attributable to Fuller's degree of involvement. The centre-piece, and arguably one of the finest sequences in the cinema, is the scene in which Joe and Charlie engage in a bout of kendo, and Joe's pent-up jealousy explodes, causing him to flout the rules and batter Charlie into unconsciousness. The ritual and stasis of the ceremonial exchanges before the bout give way to the untrammelled ferocity of Joe's attack, which is intercut with close-ups of the horrified Nisei judge whose angry face reflects the dishonour Joe has brought to their community.

Fuller has often spoken of his work in terms of journalism, even referring to certain cinematic effects as headlines. The kendo sequence is such a headline, and so is the opening evocation of Los Angeles, with rubrics flashed on the screen and the shooting of the half-naked Sugar Torch in the street. This is the world Fuller knows and understands, and his integrity in relation to it is reflected in his technique in putting it on film. Quite the contrary is true of the sequence in which Chris raises with Joe the possibility that he loves her. Chris is a painter and Joe plays the piano, and their growing involvement with each other is conveyed through a dialogue about Art. Their view of Art — and Fuller's — is a debased Romantic view compounded of Delicacy and Sadness. These sentimentalised abstractions determine the mood of the whole sequence, which accordingly lacks vitality on the part of both actors and director. Fuller is here looking at an experience from the outside. His view of art is a crass one; the view, in fact, of a crime reporter. No such problem arises in discussing *Underworld USA*, surely the most evenly realised of Fuller's films. The bleakness of its world has no room for sentimentalised abstractions.

In relation to the syndicate cycle of gangster films, *Underworld USA* is of classical purity. One man, motivated by revenge, brings down the criminal organisation and, mortally wounded, staggers from the luxurious penthouse pool where the climactic act of violence occurs, to die among the garbage cans in the alley where as a youth he watched his father being beaten to death by the men he ultimately destroys. It is the most unequivocal genre film in the Fuller canon, handling the iconography with great facility; yet it is no less personal than Fuller's other works.

Tolly Devlin (Cliff Robertson) is the typical Fuller hero, the infiltrator and double agent serving both the syndicate and the special prosecutor Driscoll, but with allegiance to neither, intent only on destroying Gela, Gunther and Smith, the men who killed his father. More clearly than any other Fuller hero, Tolly plays both ends against the middle. When Driscoll wants to pause after the destruction of Smith and Gunther, Tolly induces him to believe that Gela will co-operate with the

Newsprint as imagery in *Underworld USA*

Federal Crime Committee and at the same time convinces Connors, the boss of the syndicate, that Gela is selling him out. For Tolly the war is over after the death of Gela: he has no quarrel with Connors or the syndicate, and like Skip McCoy in *Pickup*, derides Driscoll's appeal about the defence of society. When he does decide to destroy Connors it is because of the latter's threat to his girl Cuddles. Yet once more the decision, for Fuller, makes Tolly the defender of 'a clean America'; for as Tolly drowns Connors in his swimming pool, a newspaper floating in the water makes clear the polarities in its now ironic headline 'Connors Defies Uncle Sam'.

Typically, Fuller sees the confrontation between Uncle Sam and the syndicate as a war. Driscoll, surrounded by his multi-racial staff and with mementoes of the Sixteenth Infantry Regiment decorating his walls, describes the syndicate's leaders as its 'top brass' and its activities in the imagery of military

146

strategy. Connors, too, observes that if the syndicate maintains its legitimate fronts, tax returns and charitable donations, it will 'win the war'. One of the dimensions of Fuller's hatred of war is concern with the disruptive effect it has on families. This is related to his general awareness of the vulnerability of children and concern for their education and well-being.

The final shoot-up in *House of Bamboo* occurs in a children's playground, the ex-prostitute in *The Naked Kiss* teaches in a school for crippled children, and there are orphans in *Steel Helmet*, *China Gate* and *Run of the Arrow*. But *Underworld USA* contains Fuller's most thorough response to the idea of family solidarity and children. Tolly Devlin is orphaned by three of the top men in the syndicate, and the mainspring of his motivation is loyalty to his dead father. His single-minded pursuit of revenge leads to some of the most coldly remorseless acts in the cinema: the withholding of forgiveness from the dying Vic Ferrar, the dragging of the gasping and pleading Gela to his front door to be shot down by the waiting Gus, the drowning of Connors by standing on him as he lies at the bottom of the pool. Gela observes that he wishes his son felt about him as Tolly feels about his father, and the figure of the corrupt police chief, Flower, is presented in terms of his daughter's loyalty to him when he reveals he has been 'on the take'. The threat of the syndicate's violence is most often directed against the families of its enemies, horrifically exemplified in the running down of Jenny Mencken by Gus; and ironically, the syndicate's most spectacular act of social responsibility is to throw open its swimming pool regularly to the underprivileged children of the city, with Gus acting as lifeguard.

Mother figures are common in Fuller's work (Moe in *Pickup*, Mac in *The Crimson Kimono*), but none is presented so explicitly as Sandy in *Underworld*. Unable to have children, she surrounds herself with dolls and photographs of babies, acts as a surrogate mother for Tolly as a boy by patching up his wounded face, and does the same for Cuddles, even feeding her

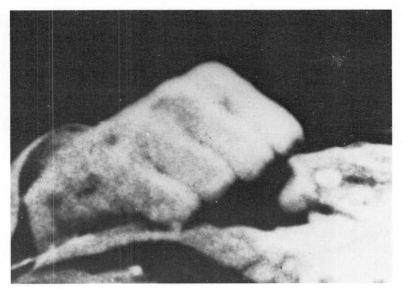

'Cinema fist': the final image of *Underworld USA*

milk. Cuddles' commitment to Tolly is expressed in her wish to have Tolly's children. The scene in which she suggests and he incredulously rejects the idea of marrying her is carefully composed round the picture of a baby above the bed.

Perhaps more than any other Hollywood director, Samuel Fuller has been ignored or reviled by Anglo-American film critics. That this is so is due undoubtedly to the brash quality of his film style (described by Peter Wollen, after Eisenstein, as 'cinema-fist'); the critics mistake a film primitive like Fuller for an impersonal, commercial hack. Yet with the possible exceptions of John Ford and Elia Kazan, no Hollywood film-maker has so consistently explored the American psyche. He deserves to be taken seriously.

149

# 12: Don Siegel

'Crime is aggressive. So is the law. Ordinary people ... don't understand the criminal's need for violence.'

Julian in *The Lineup*

One of the recurrent themes of this book is that the supposed constraints on the artist working within a commercial/industrial structure such as Hollywood may be better described as disciplines. The necessity of working within narrative and genre, with prescribed stars, a strong producer's hand and forceful collaborators, may lead not to a diminution but to an intensification of the artefact's force and range through the ironing out of its purely coterie elements. The argument could be extended to suggest that the necessity of working within fixed budgets and shooting schedules has decisively shaped the style and therefore the meaning of certain artists' work. Nowhere does this seem to have more validity than in the case of Don Siegel. In a career in feature film production which began in 1946, Siegel has, until very recently, consistently worked in the area of the so-called B-feature, always under pressure in terms of time and money. He himself reckons that these conditions have helped make his style 'taut, tight and realistic'. Siegel's demonstrably recurrent thematic concerns therefore achieve an enormously direct and forceful realisation which, in turn, draws the critic's attention to their coherence.

As Alan Lovell has pointed out in his pamphlet *Don Siegel: American Cinema*, Siegel's view of the world presupposes his heroes' rejection of or by a timorous and nondescript society, and their attempts to find an identity within a violent and

'Crime is aggressive. So is the law.' Gangsters (Mickey Rooney, Leo Gordon) and the FBI in *Baby Face Nelson*

hierarchic organisation – prison in *Riot in Cell Block 11*, the army in *Hell is for Heroes* and, most consistently, in organised crime. However, his heroes' explosive, even psychotic temperament frequently brings them into conflict with their organisations, and much of the dramatic force of Siegel's work arises from their attempts to control themselves, or be controlled by more rational associates, and to function as part of an organisation.

It is part of Siegel's artistic strategy that the organisation within which the hero tries to function is usually in opposition to another organisation, often equally hierarchic and bureaucratic. Since the Siegel hero most usually operates within organised crime, the antagonistic organisation is usually the law. The meeting-ground between them is normal society, contemptuously rejected by the criminal and ostensibly defended by the law. But Siegel's policemen seem so remote from ordinary society that its defence seems merely a pretext for their aggressive behaviour. It is difficult to conceive of Siegel's policemen having wives and families. Because the meeting-ground between the two is normal society, the criminals and the police often merge with it and scrutinise it in an attempt to identify each other. This voyeuristic exchange is encapsulated in the scene in *Baby Face Nelson* in which both sides catch sight of each other through field-glasses. In the nature of such a conflict, disguise and role-playing become supremely important, reaching a logical conclusion in *The Hanged Man*, which takes place against one of the American cinema's familiar images of concealed identity, the New Orleans Mardi Gras.

Siegel has worked within most of the manifestations of the crime film: the prison film, the juvenile delinquency film (*Crime in the Streets*), the *film policier* (*Madigan*); but his gangster films, *Baby Face Nelson* (1957), *The Lineup* (1958) and *The Killers* (1964) are among his most consistently personal, as though the genre's themes and iconography were particularly suited to his vision. Several directors have responded to different elements in the genre, and Siegel seems particularly conscious of the violent connotations of motor cars. The car chase is a recurring motif in his gangster films, present in an early and relatively impersonal film such as *The Big Steal*, appearing intermittently in *Baby Face Nelson*, and reaching its climax in *The Lineup*, which has (with the arguable exceptions of *The Big Shot* and *Bullitt*) the most exciting car chase in the genre. There are similar scenes in *Baby Face Nelson* and *The Killers*, in which policemen and gangsters are ejected from speeding cars.

*Baby Face Nelson* is one of the series of reconstructions of Thirties gangster movies characteristic of the genre in the late Fifties. However, just as Roger Corman's reconstruction *Machine-Gun Kelly* is a film incorporating the concerns of his more familiar horror films (an obsession with the paraphernalia of death and with mutilation), the title figure of *Baby Face Nelson* is discernibly in line of succession from the psychopath barely hinted at in the figure of Captain Blake (William Bendix) in *The Big Steal*, and more fully developed in the figures of Dunn (Neville Brand) and Crazy Mike Carnie (Leo Gordon) in *Riot in Cell Block 11*. Nelson's rejection of and by society is, characteristically, taken for granted, the audience being informed as Nelson leaves prison at the beginning of the film that 'society failed tragically' in his case. His instability is conveyed in his aggressiveness towards everyone he meets, in his violent love-making with Suzie (Carolyn Jones), in his manic high spirits in the bath and, most particularly, in his hysterical reaction to having killed Rocca and his men.

It is at this point that Suzie makes her first attempt to control Nelson, and reveals that her function, for Siegel, is less that of Nelson's lover than of his mentor, or rational associate, a familiar role in relation to Siegel's psychopaths in his later work. Characteristically, the disasters produced by Nelson's lack of control are linked to the unpredictability of events. Having thrown in his lot with Dillinger (played with icy calm

by Leo Gordon), Nelson is engaged with the Dillinger mob on a payroll robbery. The truck carrying the money is late and the factory whistle blows, causing Nelson to lose control and machine-gun the guards. The result is that, in the ensuing battle, a member of the gang is killed and Dillinger himself wounded. Thereafter, Nelson seems able to control himself, his ensuing acts of violence, such as killing the postman and Doc Saunders and emptying his gun against a colleague's untested bullet-proof vest, having some 'rational' basis, though his psychosis gives to these acts a frightening urgency which makes his apparent control a spurious asset. His total ruthlessness is indicated in the scene in which he prepares to machine-gun two boys who almost stumble across him in the woods – the point at which Suzie doubts the possibility of restraining him. This is the scene he recalls when, with blood dribbling from his shattered lungs, he screams at Suzie to kill him. In an outcome which Siegel was to reverse in *The Lineup*, the mentor *manqué* then kills her charge.

*The Lineup* is the most expertly constructed film in the work of a director noted for the lucidity and directness of his narrative structures. More than any other Siegel film it works out its conflicts in a series of balanced oppositions. In the conflict between the police and the criminal organisation, Siegel stresses the bureaucratic nature of the syndicate. Each member of the hierarchy has his own specialised function: the people in Far Eastern ports who place heroin in the luggage of unsuspecting travellers, the contact in San Francisco who receives photographs of the travellers, the employees among the porters and taximen on the San Francisco quayside, the collectors whose job it is to round up the packets of heroin and deliver them to 'the man', one of the syndicate's top echelon. The whole operation functions efficiently and safely because there is a minimum of contact between the syndicate's functionaries: often one does not know the identity of the other. In opposition to this, the police themselves deploy a formidable machine: hard-working and astute detectives, watchful

155

The Siegel psychopath: Mickey Rooney as Baby Face Nelson

patrolmen, forensic experts, and prowl cars which converge upon and seal off areas of the city.

The balanced opposition between the syndicate and the police is recapitulated at the level of their central representatives. Of the police pair, one provides brain, the other muscle; of the criminal pair, one provides control, the other violence. Predictably, Siegel is more interested in the criminals. Like the Mexican police captain and his subordinate in *The Big Steal*, one is teacher, the other pupil. When the two collectors arrive in San Francisco, Julian (Robert Keith) is assuring Dancer (Eli Wallach) that a proper command of the subjunctive is the mark of an educated man. Later, in a conversation with another syndicate employee, Sandy ('the best wheelman on the coast'), Julian indicates that Dancer is in the central line of succession of the Siegel hero:

*Julian:* Dancer's an addict.
*Sandy:* H as in heroin.
*Julian:* H as in hate. You never knew anyone like Dancer. He's a wonderfully pure pathological study. A psychopath with no inhibitions.

Dancer's psychosis is hinted at in his aggressive manner, but it does not become explicit until later in the film. His killings of the sailor in the steam bath and of the Chinese houseboy are controlled and efficient, the removal of obstacles to collecting the heroin. His psychosis becomes evident, in typical Siegel style, in his behaviour towards defenceless people, the little girl and her mother who brought the heroin into the country inside a doll's dress. His seizing of the child, his frantic search of the apartment and his tearing the doll to pieces (needless to say, Siegel is too sure-footed an artist to make the violatory overtones explicit) represent the beginnings of Dancer's loss of control. As in *Baby Face Nelson*, this loss of control is linked to the unpredictability of events, the little girl having used the heroin to powder her doll's face. Dancer is then forced to break the cardinal rule of the syndicate and confront 'the man' in an

*The Lineup*: Dancer (Eli Wallach), in control, shoots the Chinese houseboy

attempt to explain the loss of the heroin. The man's response, 'You're dead. You've seen my face and that makes you dead,' and the contemptuous blow he lands, drives Dancer to kill him, by which time the police are closing in. His final act of uncontrollable violence is to turn on his mentor, Julian, and kill him.

*The Lineup* offers the clearest example of the criminal organisation merging into normal society, and the consequent necessity of scrutiny this imposes on the police. The two detectives watch the director of the opera-house carefully for a trace of guilt as he examines his luggage containing the heroin; and, illustrating how closely Siegel's thematic preoccupations fit the recurrent motifs of the genre, all three watch the quayside porters as they file in for the lineup. Similarly the syndicate functionaries, representing the corporate identity of an organisation, are forced to scrutinise each other. Thus Dancer and Julian refuse, initially, to respond to Sandy's protestations that

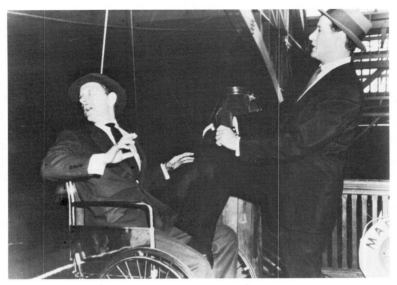

*The Lineup*: 'a psychopath with no inhibitions'; Dancer (Eli Wallach), out of control, kicks 'the man' on to the ice

he is their assigned wheelman, and all of them watch the figure of the contact at the quayside to assess his identity ('No one wears a raincoat with the collar turned down'). This remarkable scene consists of several levels of scrutiny: the initial examination of the contact, the contact's pointing out to Dancer the passengers carrying the heroin, and while this is going on, Sandy and Julian watching Dancer as they discuss his psychosis. Dancer's attempts to identify 'the man' result in a series of scrutinies of people entering the marine museum while, appropriately, Dancer pretends to be looking through a telescope. *The Lineup* has a remarkable density and overlap of thematic concerns which in no way detracts from the drive and energy of the exposition. Its coherence of theme, its lucidity, pace and elegant unity of time (the irony of Julian's recurring phrase, 'By four-thirty

ICE SKATING
SKATE RENTAL & SALES
SKATING ACCESSORIES
REST ROOMS
SPECTATORS GALLERY

it will all be over') make it the most pleasing of Siegel's films.

One situation which a film critic hopes for and so seldom finds, to have two strong directorial personalities begin from the same raw material and each produce a personal and distinctive film, occurs in the case of Ernest Hemingway's short story *The Killers*. It has twice been adapted for the screen, in 1946 by Robert Siodmak and in 1964 by Don Siegel. Each version faithfully reflects the world of its creator: Siodmak's dark, tortured and delirious, Siegel's cool, elegant and suffused with light. In the Siodmak version the killers are shadowy, functional but powerfully emblematic figures, and the unravelling of the mystery is carried out by the insurance investigator. In the Siegel version, as might be expected, the killers move to the centre of the film and conduct the investigation. Like other criminal pairs in Siegel's work, one is master, the other disciple: Charlie (Lee Marvin) cool and experienced in what he calls his profession, Lee (Clu Gulager) impulsive and admiring of the older man's expertise:

*Lee:* You know 'em all, Charlie.
*Charlie:* I'm still alive.

However, unlike Siegel's other criminal pairs, they are not so clearly differentiated into action and control. Both are capable of acts of extreme violence, as is indicated in the opening sequence, which Siegel has transposed to a blind school, the epitome of defencelessness. The manhandling which Charlie and Lee give the blind people on their way to killing Johnny North (John Cassavetes), and the cool skill of the execution, indicate both the psychosis and the precision of the killers. In particular, Charlie's sudden, berserk assault on a blind female receptionist achieves such a level of violence that, as Siegel has pointed out in an interview, no further acts of violence by Charlie are necessary to indicate his potential. Thereafter he is much more controlled, indeed decorous, than Lee, often restating questions in a lowered tone if, when first asked, they seem too imperative or violent. Hints of psychosis are thereafter carried by Lee, in his boyish good humour while on the job, in his obvious enjoyment of his work, and in his irrational tinkering with objects. The relationship between Lee and Charlie is dramatically less rich than other similar relationships in Siegel's work in the sense that possible sources of conflict between them are never explored. In a way the film is broken-backed; Siegel's primary interest is fairly clearly in the killers, but the dramatic weight of the script is on the triangular relationship of Johnny North, Jack Browning (Ronald Reagan) and Sheila Farr (Angie Dickinson), and their uncertain motives and allegiances.*

Don Siegel's style was shaped, and the themes and imagery requisite for expressing his view of the world found, within the area of the B-feature crime movie. In his more recent films, like *Madigan* (1967) and *Coogan's Bluff* (1968), the material conditions of production have changed in the sense that the budgets were larger, the shooting schedules longer and the scripts more ambitious. Significantly, both are

---

* This uncertainty in the film's structure raises a crucial question of critical method. In the chapters on individual directors in this book I have used a modified *auteur* method of criticism, that is I have offered a description of the director's recurrent thematic and/or stylistic preoccupations and related these to his gangster films and thrillers. The problem is that the *auteur* method is essentially descriptive rather than evaluative. It would have been possible simply to describe the thematic interest of Siegel's version of *The Killers*, how Charlie and Lee are recognisably Siegel figures, how like Dancer they break the rules of the organisation by finding out about the man they killed, how disguise enters the film in the mail robbery and so on. However, it seems also an important critical exercise to work out why *The Killers* is an inferior film to, say, *The Lineup*, and for this the critic needs a different method which involves assessing the strategy of the individual film and the extent to which this is coherently realised. I have no doubt that these methods are complementary and not, as some critics would have it, conflicting. The *auteur* method, with its stress on looking at all a director's films, can yield valuable information about what, precisely, the director's preoccupations are. There its usefulness ends and structural scrutiny of individual films must begin.

The price of curiosity: Charlie (Lee Marvin) pays it in *The Killers*

crime movies, their central figures bear many of the marks of previous Siegel heroes, and stylistically there is much of the lucidity and pace of earlier films. It is rather too early to tell, but it is to be hoped that changed conditions of production will leave unimpaired the coherence and directness of Siegel's work.

# 13: Jean-Pierre Melville

'At birth man is offered only one choice – the choice of his death. But if this choice is governed by distaste for his own existence, his life will never have been more than meaningless.'

Prologue to *Le Deuxième Souffle*

One of the most bizarre, and potentially unrewarding, phenomena the film critic must confront is the genre which has been transplanted from one culture to another. If his critical orientation is pro-*auteur* and anti-genre, or pro-'art' and anti-'popular' cinema, he is likely to reject genre transplantation as arid and synthetic. This view, however, oversimplifies the situation with regard to American genres transplanted to Europe. Much of the continuing vitality of the Western is arguably due to the efforts of the Italian director Sergio Leone; and unquestionably the most interesting figure now working in the gangster film is the Frenchman, Jean-Pierre Melville.

The French cinema had, of course, its own native history in the crime film: a fantasy tradition going back to the serials of Louis Feuillade, and a relatively more realistic tradition dating from the Marcel Carné/Julien Duvivier films of the late Thirties. However, Raymonde Borde and Etienne Chaumeton, in their *Panorama du Film Noir Américain*, regard André Hunebelle's *Mission à Tanger* (1949) as the first French *film noir* discernibly influenced by American models, and the years 1954-55 as the high-water mark of such influence, with an American actor, Eddie Constantine, dominating the scene as Lemmy Caution. Borde and Chaumeton stress the unsatisfactory, parodic* quality of the films of this period, and regard the French *film noir* of the time as being best exemplified by two gangster films, Jacques Becker's *Touchez Pas au Grisbi* (1953) and Jules Dassin's *Rififi* (1955). Both these films, centrally concerned with loyalty and betrayal in the underworld, point forward to the superb canon of Jean-Pierre Melville.

Melville's background and career crystallise a whole set of problems for the Anglo-American film critic. On the one hand, there is Melville the French intellectual, adaptor of books by Vercors, Jean Cocteau and Béatrix Beck. On the other there is Melville the Americanophile, admirer of Hollywood, adopting his name from the greatest of American novelists, and maker of six gangster films, some of them at least solidly within the taste and experience of a wide popular audience and, arguably, much more personal (i.e. reflecting his universe) than his literary adaptations. These two Melvilles exist in the same man without any sense of strain. Indeed, the implication of his career is that art, defined as the creation of a coherent personal world, exists in the 'commercial' rather than in the 'art' cinema, a precept much preached by the *Cahiers* group when they were critics but little practised by them as film-makers.

Melville's gangster or related films are *Bob le Flambeur* (1955), *Deux Hommes dans Manhattan* (1958), *Le Doulos* (1962), *L'Aîné des Ferchaux* (1962), *Le Deuxième Souffle* (1965) and *Le Samourai* (1967). Of these, only *Le Deuxième Souffle* is currently available for study in Britain. The Bressonian escape from prison with which the film opens (there is more than a superficial similarity between Melville's and Bresson's work) releases Gustave Minda (Lino Ventura), an aging gangster, into a uniquely Melvillian world. Gu's central problem is whether he is capable of fitting into the milieu he left ten years before. The rewards of this world are loyalty and a loving tenderness from friends, its obligations the highest

---

* The use made by French film-makers of their involvement with Hollywood has often been flippant, as in Godard's *A Bout de Souffle* and *Bande à Part*, and Truffaut's *Tirez sur le Pianiste*.

*Le Deuxième Souffle*: the 'impassive mastery' of Gu Minda (Lino Ventura)

professional skill and a similar loyalty in return. The themes of loyalty, tenderness and professionalism, the mainsprings of the film, are interpenetrated in the texture of the narrative.

The theme of loyalty is expressed early in terms of the relationship between Manouche (Gu's woman) and her bodyguard, Alban. Alban's loyalty is demonstrated in innumerable services, but it achieves its most profound statement in the sequence in which Manouche is menaced by two hoods and one of them, sticking a gun in Alban's back, orders him to call her. He answers with an impassive negative shake of the head and is brutally clubbed. Alban's loyalty is quite naturally offered to Gu, again in innumerable services such as bringing things Gu needs to his hideout and, most strikingly, before Gu's departure for Marseilles, in giving Gu the gun from which he has never previously been separated. The theme of loyalty is restated throughout the film, in Orloff's complete assurance that Gu's skills are intact after ten years in prison, in his suggesting Gu as the fourth man to join the bullion robbery, in Paul Ricci's ready acceptance of Gu for the job, and in Gu's immediate readiness to participate when he learns it is being organised by Paul. The texture of interdependence created in the first half of the film, as well as expressing a central theme, has a dramatic function in explaining Gu's reaction (he goes berserk and tries to kill himself) to Commissaire Fardiano's spreading of the lie that he has betrayed his comrades in the bullion hold-up. Ultimately Gu destroys himself proving his loyalty.

It might be expected that the most tender relationship in the film would be between Gu and Manouche. A tenderness certainly exists between them, but in an overall impression of the film the most memorable acts of tenderness are between Gu and other men. At the beginning, the man with whom Gu escapes helps him board a goods train, gives him a cigarette, lays his hand on his shoulder in a protective gesture, and jumps off the train again to disappear into the forest. Similarly, there are innumerable embraces in the film, between Gu and Frank, Gu and Orloff, and moments when men touch each other gently – as Gu touches Antoine's shoulder after the robbery – which are not homosexual in the usual sense of the term, but are rather expressive of respect, admiration, loyalty. The relationship of Commissaire Blot, the central police figure, to the criminal world is analogous to this. He has an easy relationship with Jo Ricci and Alban, perhaps even loves Manouche, and describes Gu's technique in killing the two hoods who menaced Manouche as 'the mark of a master'. After Gu's death, Blot even places Fardiano's confession – that he had lied about Gu betraying his friends – in the hands of the Press. It is as though Blot were observing the rules of a game in which he and the underworld are on different sides without any personal malice existing between them.

The figures in *Le Deuxième Souffle* earn the love and loyalty of their friends by their intense professionalism, which is demonstrated primarily by four men: Gu, Orloff, Antoine and

'Loyalty and tenderness': Denis Manuel and Lino Ventura in *Le Deuxième Souffle*

Blot. Gu in action as he kills the two hoods, Fardiano and the motorcycle policeman, displays a terse and impassive mastery. The theme of professionalism is carried strikingly in the self-sufficient figure of Orloff, who prefers to work alone but who, sometime in the past, has earned the love and loyalty of Paul and Gu. Orloff's professionalism is inherent in his cautious casing of Frank Ricci's house before entering it to receive the invitation to take part in the bullion robbery; Antoine's is demonstrated in his killing of the motorcycle escort. The narrative brilliantly sets these figures in opposition, resulting in one of the two set-pieces of the film (the other is the robbery itself). Having arranged to meet Antoine, Pascal and Jo Ricci to listen to their complaints about Gu, Orloff goes to the rendezvous some time before the meeting and plants a gun in the most convenient concealed place, on top of a cupboard. Antoine goes there shortly after him, tests each chair for the overall view and potential control of the scene it offers, and discovers the concealed gun. When trouble threatens at the meeting, Orloff ignores the gun he has planted and produces a gun, as if by magic, from his coat, revealing that he had intended Antoine to find the gun on top of the cupboard.

Blot, too, is a strikingly professional figure: in the *tour de force* at the beginning of the film when, arriving at Manouche's restaurant to investigate the shooting of Jacques, he ironically forecasts the staff's account of the incident; in his knowing that Gu is likely to try to kill Jo Ricci; in his hunch that both the killing of the two hoods and of the motorcycle policeman were done by Gu; and in his final trick to get Gu to reveal his complicity in the robbery.

Melville's handling of the gangster film is analogous to Sergio Leone's handling of the Western: that is, both push the genres to a remarkable degree of stylisation. This is expressed in Melville's work primarily at the basic level of iconography. He exercises extreme care in the casting, dress and deportment of his players. Both Lino Ventura and Michel Constantin (Alban) were associated with the French gangster film before working with Melville, and they and Pierre Zimmer (Orloff) have enormous force simply as shapes on the screen, Ventura in the emblematic trench-coat which recalls both Humphrey Bogart and Alan Ladd. The most striking feature of *Le Deuxième Souffle* is the degree of impassivity Melville imposes on his players, which gives them remarkable dignity and strength.

Retrospectively, the theme of the necessity of human contact, of friendship at whatever price, seems extremely important in Melville's work. The German officer in *Le Silence de la Mer* causes the young French girl to fall in love with him by his dignified bearing in the face of her uncle's total silence towards him; the priest in *Léon Morin, Prêtre* runs the risk of letting a young widow fall in love with him, ostensibly for the sake of her soul, but arguably for the human friendship she offers him; and, of course, expressions of friendship and love form a recurrent motif of *Le Deuxième Souffle*.

168

'Stylised impassivity': Jacques Leroy and Alain Delon in *Le Samourai*

However, all these impulses to human contact are the reverse of the coin of another powerful impulse in Melville's work, the awareness of human isolation. The impassivity of his actors is matched by the sense of formal stasis in his work, which frequently makes itself manifest in the repeated image of a figure isolated in the centre of the frame and inhabiting an empty or near-empty room. This image is particularly powerful in *Léon Morin, Prêtre* and in *L'Armée des Ombres* (1969), Melville's account of the Resistance, and is present, too, in *Le Deuxième Souffle*. The theme that this image expresses, however, receives its most single-minded statement in *Le Samourai*. Where Gu Minda is surrounded by friends who consistently help him, and defines his own value by what his friends think of him, Jeff Costello (Alain Delon), the hired killer in *Le Samourai*, is entirely alone, connecting with Gu only at the level of his superb professionalism. The casting is important here. Lino Ventura carries in his physical presence the qualities of force and decisiveness necessary for the role of Gu, but his physical presence does not exclude the possibility of love and friendship. Delon, on the other hand, has one of the coldest personae on the screen. Antonioni, it will be recalled, cast him in *L'Eclisse* because 'his face is harsh and pitiless'.

Thematically, therefore, *Le Samourai* is the bleakest and most austere of Melville's films, its central figure pushed to a remarkable degree of stylised impassivity. Many of the most characteristic moments of the film involve Costello alone in his room, lying on the bed before going out to fulfil his contract, as in the opening sequence, dressing a wounded arm (Melville's interest in the *process* of doing things probably stems from his admiration for Jacques Becker's *Le Trou*), or searching for a microphone concealed in his room by the police. Such relationships as Jeff is seen to have, as with Jane Lagrange (Nathalie Delon), are cold and opportunistic, and even his relationship with the Police Chief (François Périer) has none of the humour or mutual admiration which characterise the dealings between Gu and Blot in *Le Deuxième Souffle*. Stylistically the film is also extremely austere. The fact that it is in colour raises expectations that its emotional range might be more extreme than earlier black and white Melville movies, but so controlled, so muted is the colour that it has the opposite effect of stressing the thematic austerity. It is shot largely at night (Melville has often said that films about cities should begin at sunset and end at dawn) and in the opening sequence in Jeff's darkened room, Melville has taken the trouble to mute all sources of colour; the label on a bottle of Vichy water, the Gauloise cigarette packet, the banknotes, are all grey/black photocopies of the brightly coloured originals.

If the theme of *Le Samourai* leads to a film of great stylistic austerity, this is perhaps at some expense in dramatic force. This is best exemplified by comparing analogous scenes in *Le Samourai* and *Le Deuxième Souffle*: the placing of the microphone in Jeff's room by the police and his subsequent discovery of it, and the planting of the gun at the rendezvous by Orloff and its discovery by Antoine. In the former, two faceless police-men, whom the audience has not previously met and will not meet again, enter Jeff's room, carefully reconnoitre it and plant the bug (Melville, with his usual interest in process, showing us every detail). Jeff comes back, senses that something is amiss from the restlessness of his budgerigar, and tracks the bug down, Melville again stressing the process. There is a similar interest in process in the parallel scene from *Le Deuxième Souffle*, but here both Antoine and Orloff are known to the audience, Melville has set up their antagonism earlier in the film, and he withholds the information that Orloff has foreseen that Antoine will discover the gun until, in the showdown, Orloff ignores the gun he has planted (and Antoine removed) and goes for the gun in his pocket. The fact that the audience knows Orloff and Antoine and their antagonism, plus the revelation Melville makes about Orloff's supreme skill and professionalism, give this sequence a dramatic force almost totally absent from the analogous sequence in *Le Samourai*.

*Le Samourai* functions very markedly within the traditions of the gangster film. Once again, the iconography of dress is stressed and, even more than *Bob le Flambeur* or *Deux Hommes dans Manhattan*, it has a sense of the city, of rain-soaked streets, of automobiles, of early-morning lineups in police stations, of luxury apartments and cheap rooming-houses, of expensive night-clubs. In the context of the gangster film, Melville is important for two reasons: as a measuring rod of the extent of the American cinema's influence on the French film, and as a figure who, starting out within the tradition of the 'art' cinema, found his most congenial means of expression in the popular cinema. The future of the gangster film could not lie in better hands.

'. . . a figure isolated in the centre of the frame.' Serge Reggiani in *Le Doulos*

# Acknowledgements

Stills are by courtesy of Warner Bros., 20th Century-Fox, Paramount, Columbia, MGM, United Artists, Rank, Gala, Universal, British Lion, RKO, Republic, Jean-Pierre Melville and the National Film Archive.

Thanks are due to Alan Lovell, Peter Wollen, Ian Leslie Christie, Dan Millar and Colin Shindler, all of whom read and commented on parts of the manuscript; Tom Milne and David Wilson, who were sympathetic editors; Sue Bennett and Georges Cohen for translations from the French; David Austen, Eddie Patman and Barry Hindson for help with stills; Linda Woolf and Susan Reed for typing parts of the manuscript; and David Meeker for arranging screenings of inaccessible films.

This book is dedicated to my mother and late father.

C. McA.

# General index

174

# Index of film titles